What if...

Everyone Was Doing It

a choose
your destiny
NOVEL

What if...
Everyone Was Doing It

LIZ RUCKDESCHEL AND SARA JAMES

DELACORTE PRESS

Published by Delacorte Press
an imprint of Random House Children's Books
a division of Random House, Inc.
New York

This is a work of fiction. Names, characters, places, and
incidents either are the product of the author's imagination or are
used fictitiously. Any resemblance to actual persons, living or
dead, events, or locales is entirely coincidental.

Text copyright © 2008 by Liz Ruckdeschel and Sara James

Delacorte Press and colophon are registered trademarks of
Random House, Inc.

Visit us on the Web! www.randomhouse.com/teens
www.thewhatifbooks.com

Educators and librarians, for a variety of teaching tools,
visit us at www.randomhouse.com/teachers

Library of Congress Cataloging-in-Publication Data

Ruckdeschel, Liz.
What if—everyone was doing it : a choose your destiny novel / by Liz
Ruckdeschel and Sara James. — 1st ed.
p. cm.
Summary: As Haley's first spring break from Hillsdale High comes to an
end, she continues to try to find her place there, while the reader's
choices help her to select boyfriends, sports, and other activities,
as well as how to juggle her busy schedule.
ISBN 978-0-385-73502-5 (trade edition) — ISBN 978-0-385-90496-4
(glb edition) 1. Plot-your-own stories. [1. Popularity—Fiction. 2. High
schools—Fiction. 3. Schools—Fiction. 4. Plot-your-own stories.]
I. James, Sara. II. Title.
PZ7.R842Whc 2007
[Fic]—dc22
2007035617

The text of this book is set in 12.5-point Apollo MT.

Printed in the United States of America

10 9 8 7 6 5 4 3 2 1

First Edition

SPRING FEVER

Fever is often accompanied by a chill.

To Haley Miller, there was nothing worse than getting close to a friend or a boy only to then be snubbed. It was twice as bad as someone not liking you in the first place. Which was why she found it so incredibly unacceptable that *certain* people in Hillsdale were now avoiding her after she had spent almost all of spring break with them.

What is going on? Haley thought, baffled as to why no one was returning her e-mails or phone calls.

Fortunately, Haley had something to distract her.

The Miller family was driving down to Pennsylvania to celebrate Easter Sunday at her grandmother Polly's horse farm, Penn Ultimate. Gam called it that because, as she said, "This is the second-to-last place I want to go before I die. After that, it better be the pearly gates of heaven."

But to Haley, Penn Ultimate was paradise itself. Gam's squat yellow farmhouse and old red barn were tucked between a fruit orchard and a horse pasture where three palominos were usually grazing, snorting or stamping their hooves in the rich brown dirt. A spring-fed swimming hole sat at one edge of the property, and there was a vegetable garden in the backyard. Fresh milk and eggs were delivered twice weekly by neighboring farmers.

Haley had yet to encounter such perfection anywhere else on earth—at least, not in the few parts of the world she had seen so far. In fact, the only things Haley could have done *without* at Gam Polly's were the old knitting needles, pattern books and yarn spools packed into one of the spare-bedroom closets. Considering the harm Gam Polly could inflict with her chosen craft, the knitting supplies were about as terrifying as if Gam kept a closet full of rusty knives and meat hooks. Even so, the prospect of two nights at Penn Ultimate was tantalizing—almost enough to make Haley forget that her cell phone refused to vibrate. *Almost.*

"Here we are!" Perry Miller, Haley's dad, exclaimed as he pulled up the drive in the family's hybrid SUV. Freckles, the Millers' overeager Dalmatian, was the first to bound out of the car. He barked excitedly, did a few laps around the house, then rolled on the lawn with Gam's black Scottie dog, Arthur, as Haley and her little brother, Mitchell, got out to stretch their legs.

"Do you. Think. Gam. Has been knitting. Since Christmas," Mitchell asked Haley in a deliberate monotone. Mitchell had insisted on talking like a robot for almost a year now, and Haley had sort of gotten used to it.

"Sorry, Mitchie," Haley replied, pulling her straight auburn hair into a bun. "But I think we must *always* assume that Gam Polly has been knitting."

Joan Miller got out of the front seat holding a picnic basket overflowing with home-baked goods. "Can I offer anyone a snack?" she asked brightly. Ever since Haley's mom had won her recent toxic torts lawsuit, she had been fervently devoting herself to her family to make up for the "lost months" she had spent on her case.

Perry too had recently completed his latest project, a three-years-in-the-making documentary on the life cycle of deciduous trees. Needless to say, there was a lot more Miller togetherness these days.

"Well, finally," Gam said, descending the front

steps in a gray quilted jacket, gardening gloves and dark blue dungarees. "I thought we might have to send out a search party."

"Who. Is that," Mitchell asked Haley as they caught a glimpse of a smiling, gray-haired gentleman standing sheepishly on the porch.

Gam cast a glance over her shoulder. "Oh, that's just Harvey Pickleman," she declared in her typical no-nonsense way while giving Haley and Mitchell a good squeeze. "He lives next door. We play backgammon sometimes."

"What is. A pickle man," Mitchell asked, still eyeing Harvey suspiciously. Haley too was curious. *So this must be the reason Gam had to race back to Pennsylvania after Christmas,* she thought, recalling her grandmother's hasty departure in the middle of the Miller family meltdown.

"I'm not sure I know what a pickleman is, Mitchell," said Gam. "All I can tell you is, that fellow over there don't know a cucumber from a zucchini." She cracked a smile and boomed, "Now, Perry, come give your old mother a hug."

Haley watched as her grandmother shot Joan a disapproving look over Perry's shoulder. Gam had been in Hillsdale during the worst of Joan's workaholic phase, and she wasn't about to let her daughter-in-law forget it, even if the rest of the family had already forgiven and forgotten.

"Come on into the house," Gam said finally,

rounding up the Miller crew. "I've got fried chicken and potato salad for lunch, and I just might be persuaded to make some ice cream before supper." Gam charged through the front door, leaving Harvey to make his own introductions.

Yep, Haley thought, approaching Mr. Pickleman to shake his hand, *this is going to be one interesting trip.*

It took approximately three hours for Harvey to win over Haley and Mitchell, which also happened to be exactly how long it took them to learn he was an ace at Ping-Pong. From that point on, Gam's sunroom was transformed into a competitive arena, with Harvey stationed at one end of the bright green table. He faced each of the kids across the net before besting Perry, who considered Ping-Pong a sport worthy of Olympic-level concentration.

It wasn't until Easter Sunday, however, that Haley and Mitchell came to really adore Harvey. On that morning, Haley, who had been through enough holidays with Gam to know better, looked skeptically at her Easter present. The box was large enough to contain all manner of knitted catastrophes, and Haley's heart raced as she considered the possibilities. Steeling herself, she gingerly pulled off the lid. Inside the box, nestled in folds of tissue paper, she found . . . an actual straight-from-the-department-store dress! And a pretty cute one, at that. The fabric was black linen, and it had a scoop neck, a fitted bodice and a fullish skirt. "Wow, Gam, thank you. I love it!" Haley exclaimed with a mixture of amazement and profound relief. She lunged to hug her grandmother, who kept her composure, as usual.

"Harvey helped me pick it out," Gam said sternly. "You know how I feel about store-bought presents."

Haley glanced over at Harvey and smiled as he gave her a conspiratorial wink. She wondered briefly if the Millers had finally seen the last of Gam's knitted masterpieces.

Unfortunately for Mitchell, they had not. Haley's brother tore into his package expectantly, only to uncover a bright blue knitted Easter Bunny costume, complete with big floppy ears, a white belly and . . . footies. "Oh. No," Mitchell said flatly.

"That's right, sporto, you get to be the Easter Bunny this year," Gam said, beaming. "Well, come on, now. Don't be shy. Why don't you go and put it on for us?" Mitchell, who normally didn't show much emotion on his face, looked horrified.

"Ahem, Pollykins—" Harvey began, with a hint of reproach in his voice. "Remember what we talked about earlier?" The color rose in Gam's cheeks. Haley couldn't tell if this was because Harvey had just called her grandmother by an apparent nickname or because he was scolding her in front of the family. "I think what your Gam meant to say, Mitchell, is that this bunny suit is really more for sleeping in," Harvey continued. "You don't have to wear it in public if you don't want to."

Haley felt like bowing down at Harvey's feet. And from the look in her brother's eyes, so did Mitchell.

The hardest part of coming to Penn Ultimate was always leaving Penn Ultimate. Haley and Mitchell moped all afternoon as the family packed up their belongings and loaded the car. "When will. I. See you. Again," Mitchell asked as Gam gave him a squeeze goodbye.

"You just say the word, kiddo, and I'll be there," Gam said, looking harshly at Joan. "New Jersey's not that far."

"It is. Exactly. One hundred. And seven. Point three. Miles," Mitchell replied.

Gam looked surprised. She knelt down and looked Mitchell in the eye. "You know, I think a boy old enough to know his geography is maybe getting too old for my knitted pajamas."

"Affirmative."

Haley was stunned. She turned to her father and whispered, "But who will Gam knit for now?"

"Oh, don't worry," Perry whispered back. "One of my cousins just had triplets."

Haley smiled. Besides, she thought, looking at Harvey, Gam had other things to concern herself with these days.

"Oh, stop," Gam said, shrugging Harvey off as he

tried to put his arm around her. "What will the children think?"

Haley, for one, thought Harvey Pickleman was pretty great.

With each roll of the tires toward home on that one-hundred-and-seven-point-three-mile trip, Haley's thoughts returned to Hillsdale and her friends—or lack thereof. Through farm country, cellular service was spotty at best, but every time Haley got a signal, she was reminded that the texts and voice mails weren't exactly pouring in.

When she got home, there were only two e-mails waiting for her: a mass e-mail from an anonymous Hillsdale High sender, suggesting that something major had happened between Annie Armstrong and Dave Metzger on their trip to Spain over spring break, and a class announcement stating that Irene Chen had been selected to design the yearbook cover.

Haley had never felt so neglected in her life. No one had ever frozen her out like this before. And she was determined to find out why, starting first thing in the morning when she headed back to school.

• • •

Poor Haley Miller. Just as she was settling in at Hillsdale High, they go and push her back out. Has all Haley's progress vanished overnight? And if so, what has she done to deserve this banishment to social Siberia?

Haley's next step is your call. Since she has no

invitations to accept or decline, and right now, no one seems to care whether she lives or dies, she'll have to ease back into the scene at school. So which e-mail do you think piqued Haley's curiosity? Would she rather find out what happened between Annie and Dave over spring break? Or is she more excited/annoyed that Irene Chen gets to design this year's *Talon* cover? If the announcement about Irene and the yearbook seems more interesting, turn to THE NEW COVER GIRL on page 16. If you think Haley is more intrigued by the rumors about Dave and Annie, turn to EUROPEAN UNIONS on page 10.

Behavior can be contagious in school. And right now, the thing to do at Hillsdale High seems to be shunning Haley Miller. So what if ... everyone was doing something? That is, everyone except you?

Once you've been abroad,
you're no longer a little girl.

Haley had loved spending her spring break in Europe with her friends. But between that and the whirlwind Easter trip to Gam Polly's, she felt as if she had been gone from school at least a month. In her absence, it was as if the whole social order at Hillsdale High had realigned. And once again, Haley had to figure out where she fit in.

She could only assume that her traveling companions hadn't been quite as psyched as she'd been about their daily walks down cobblestone streets and adventures in outdoor markets. The longer Haley's cell phone went without ringing, the more paranoid she became. *Was I too chatty on the plane?* she wondered. *Did I bring too much luggage and slow everyone down? Was it because I used my map in public and asked that cute guy for directions?* Worse still, she thought, *Did I have bad breath or BO?*

Haley couldn't figure it out.

Eerily, the courtyard where her friends normally spent time between classes was empty. *Great,* she thought, *they so don't want to see me that they've abandoned our usual hangout.* Haley plopped down on a bench and moped.

"Are you looking for your friends?" a pretty brunette asked, smacking her gum. "They're in the rotunda. That's where all the cool kids go once spring starts. Duh."

"Where's the rotunda?" Haley asked, frowning.

"Out by the math wing," the girl said, nodding in the direction of that dreaded architectural maze, which had baffled and sabotaged so many Hillsdale students over the years.

Haley took a moment to adjust to the fact that someone thought of her as a cool kid. No matter that it was a bratty little freshman. "Um, okay, thanks," Haley said.

"No prob . . . Haley," the girl said, twirling a strand of hair with her finger. So the freshman knew her name. Haley stood up and headed in the general direction of the math wing as the girl called after her, "I'm Candy. Candy Davenport."

Like I care, Haley thought.

After following the perimeter of the building, then stopping and retracing her steps—twice— Haley was about to give up and head to first period alone. But then an archway caught her eye. She veered left, turned a corner and finally emerged in a large *en plein air* rotunda lined with budding trees, where a few dozen kids were clustered around some stone tables and benches. Haley looked around, amazed. She'd been a student at Hillsdale High for almost a full school year now, and she had never even caught a glimpse of this place.

There was Sasha Lewis, looking very much like a girl who had just returned from Paris. She was standing amid a group of admirers, wearing a tank top, black heels and jeans, her blond hair looking mussed and slept-on. Sasha's gorgeous boyfriend, Johnny Lane, was, as usual, right by her side, the epitome of a louche French rocker. He had on cords, a faded red vintage T-shirt, a black blazer and black low-top sneakers. Haley could overhear Sasha telling some fabulous story about how they had gotten separated in a Parisian nightclub and reconnected on the dance floor.

At the next table, a crowd had gathered around Annie Armstrong and Dave Metzger, who were still sun kissed from their Spanish holiday. Annie's up-tight cardigans, braids and past-the-knee skirts had been replaced by a flowing, embroidered goddess dress, loose curls and high-heeled sandals. Dave, meanwhile, was speaking in a voice that was a full octave lower than the shy, cracked staccato known and loved by fans of his podcast, "Inside Hillsdale." He also seemed to be standing up straighter, and his hair, Haley could've sworn, wasn't nearly as wiry and frizzled as when he'd left. *Is Dave wearing* prod-uct? she marveled, aghast.

Haley couldn't quite put her finger on it, but something had definitely changed about Hillsdale's straight-A goody-goodies since they'd come back from Seville. And she, along with half the people in the courtyard, couldn't wait to find out what had caused their transformation.

Haley looked down at her own outfit. In all her angst that morning over why she hadn't heard from her friends, she hadn't paid any mind to her clothes. Seeing the old chinos, holey white cardigan and blue flats she'd thrown on, she felt, well, sort of plain, especially next to these women of the world. After Haley had been standing there a full three minutes, Annie and Sasha both looked up, no-ticed her and gave a half smile and a weak wave. Haley weighed her options, deciding who to ap-proach first.

What's with the spring break afterglow? All these couples seem to have come back from Europe looking extra lovey-dovey.

Annie and Dave are definitely radiating a new kind of energy. So what's up? Did they finally hook up in Spain? And is Haley ready to find out if they went all the way?

What about Sasha and Johnny? Has their trip to Paris and new status as bandmates in the Hedon solidified them as a couple? Or will too much togetherness start to tear them apart?

What about the girl who normally dominates sophomore-class social functions, Coco De Clerq? Why is she nowhere in sight?

And finally, where have all the boys gone? Sebastian was in Spain with Annie and Dave, and Reese Highland made the trip to Europe with Sasha and Johnny, so where are they now? And who do you think Haley would rather see?

To have Haley choose to hang with the rock 'n' rollers, Sasha and Johnny, where there's a good possibility she'll run into Reese, flip to CAFETERIA on page 24. If you think Hillsdale's newest movers and shakers, Annie and Dave, are far more interesting now that they're world travelers, have Haley volunteer to help them out at the yearbook committee meeting after school on page 31 (RULE BY COMMITTEE). Alternatively, since

Haley's friends have been ignoring her, should she blow them off too? If so, skip ahead and have her find out what Coco De Clerq is up to in IN THE SWING on page 40.

It's tough being the odd girl out, but only if you're always dying to get back in.

THE NEW COVER GIRL

Models aren't the only ones who can land a cover.

On the first day back at school after spring break, Haley spotted some of the artsy kids from her grade hanging out in the parking lot. She watched as two girls with sunburned faces, blond cornrows and Bob Marley T-shirts walked past Shaun Willkommen and Irene Chen.

"Yah, Jamaica spring break, mon," Shaun mocked. Haley noticed he had shed a little weight since his motocross Valentine's Day stunt, which had put him in the hospital and temporarily destroyed his senses of taste and smell. Shaun's blond mullet had also been singed in said accident, and now he wore a crewcut that better complemented his face. "Very original, kitties," he added.

"Whatever, Willkommen," one of the girls snapped. "At least we left Hillsdale over break."

"Um, at least we're leaving Hillsdale after high school," Irene retorted. "Enjoy that job at the mall, Kirsten."

Just then, Garrett "the Troll" Noll rolled past them on his skateboard. "You gotta admit, it is pretty lame you guys stayed here the whole time," he said, patting the top of Irene's green newsboy cap so that it covered her eyes.

"Yeah, dude," added a kid known only as Chopper. He shoved Garrett off the skateboard and took a pass through the parking lot himself. "Even *we* got out of town," he added, grinding the board along the edge of a curb.

"Yooo doggies! Did we ever. Took our earnings from the garden center and drove down to Panama City, *F-L-A*," the Troll added, clearly impressed with his own ingenuity. "All the coeds we could handle." He held out his arms and pretended he was making out with not one but three girls.

"Right," said Irene. "Like a college girl would come within ten feet of you two."

"Seriously," Chopper chimed in, "they was all over us."

Shaun and Irene looked at each other and simultaneously rolled their eyes. Haley debated whether to approach. Her cell phone had been silent for four days, and between that and her empty e-mail in-box, she was unusually paranoid about talking to *anyone* at school. Even Shaun and Irene.

"Panama City," Irene began in an even harsher tone than usual, "is a pastel-colored wasteland. I went there once with my parents. Just a bunch of fish shacks with purply drinks, and a bunch of vomit on the street."

Haley decided that, for the moment, at least, maybe it was best to keep her distance from Irene.

"If you must know, we *elected* to remain in the greater metropolis of Hillsdale for the duration of our time off," Shaun said in an affected accent.

" 'Time off'?" challenged Irene. "Speak for yourself, white man. I worked doubles all week at the G. D. and stayed up nights to finish my graphic novel, *The Jade Lily*."

" 'Rini," Shaun began. Haley guessed this was his new pet name for Irene. "It totally paid off. We had this little art show at my place," he boasted to Chopper and Troll, "and my mom's Chelsea gallery friend was way into Irene's renderings."

"Seriously?" asked Chopper.

"Totes," said Shaun. "Harold Greene. Is da king. Of the art scene. Greene machine. And now Mr. Von has asked Irene to design the cover of this year's *Talon*."

"Shaun," Irene said sternly. Haley knew this was not a girl who liked being bragged about. "That Harold guy never called, and I don't think it's such an honor to be forced to hang out with Annie Armstrong and all the other uptight, all-we-care-about-is-deadlines geeks on the yearbook committee. But thanks for reminding me how I'm going to be spending the next few weeks. Awesome."

"Dude, if you design the cover of the yearbook, you're pretty much, like, guaranteed to become a household name," Chopper marveled, sounding jealous.

"Like where? At Hillsdale High?" Irene asked sarcastically. "Um, no thanks."

"But people keep their high school yearbooks for, like, e-vah," added Chopper. "Even my parents still have theirs. And that thing is crazy. They're all in bell-bottoms and big square glasses. Man, I wish they'd kept some of that stuff."

The Troll skated by. "Aren't you in charge of designing posters for the Battle of the Bands too?" he asked Irene.

She forced a smile. "Come see the Hedon, with Hillsdale's hottest rocker couple, Sasha Lewis and Johnny Lane, as they square off against—who else?—Rubber Dynamite! Cue the screaming girls and drooling jocks. How do I get myself into these things?"

The Troll nodded in agreement. "Dude, Johnny has totally crossed over. He's one of them now. Even scored himself a wanted babe. I bet we won't see him out here for the rest of the semester."

Irene frowned. "How do you know?"

Haley thought Shaun looked hurt, but he quickly recovered.

"Man, where's the Devster?" Chopper asked him. Haley's ears perked up. She too was curious to know where the cute photographer Devon McKnight was hiding himself post–spring break.

"Am I my homey's keeper?" asked Shaun.

"He's dealing with family stuff," Irene explained.

"Well, he was supposed to be filming me hopping trash cans in the parking lot," Chopper said. "What could be more important than that?"

"I'll race you," Shaun said as he picked up his pogo stick. He began to bounce up and down. "Time to prove I got the sporto groove," he said, and bounced onto the curb and back down to the pavement. "Did I tell you dweezils I'm trying out for track and field?"

"I thought participation in athletics was against your religion," Chopper replied.

"I'm hurdling a loophole, my friend," Shaun said, bouncing even higher. "My gold shorts gonna be javelin' the throw, vaultin' the pole and a-puttin' the shot." He pretended to launch an object into the air. "Heads up, girlies!" he yelled, causing a cluster of freshmen to scatter, terrified something was about to fall on them.

Irene smiled. "If you're going to join a sport, track and field is actually pretty cool," she said.

"Personally, I get all the exercise I need skateboarding," the Troll said before wiping out on a bump in the asphalt.

"Dude, you've got gravel in your chin," Chopper said, eyes wide as he examined the Troll's open wound. "Where the heck is Devon with his camera when you need him?"

"Holy shiitake mushroom," Irene said, catching a glimpse of the hard-court playing surface that was adjacent to the parking lot, though separated by a tall chain-link fence. "Speaking of organized sports. Isn't that Coco De Clerq? With . . . a . . . tennis racket?"

"Well, well, well, look who found John McEnroe over spring break," said Shaun.

"Don't laugh," Irene replied. "Worshiping at the altar of the superbrat is probably the closest Coco will ever come to finding a deity."

They all watched in awe as the former teen queen and star of the Hillsdale High sophomore class grunted and lunged and chased down balls. Coco was a mess. Her face was beet red; her tennis whites were covered in grime. Clearly, she'd been at this for hours. And still she swung at ball after ball with her backhand, forehand and overhead lob, whipping them back across the net to the tennis coach.

"Since when does Her Hillsdale Highness . . . *sweat*?" Chopper marveled, half grossed out and half smitten.

"She's not so bad, I guess," said a confident voice coming from directly behind Haley. "Now if only someone would help her get a net game."

Haley spun around to find Spencer Eton flashing his trademark cocky grin. "Am I . . . interrupting?" he asked, looking at Haley, then at Shaun and Irene's group a short distance away.

"How long have you been standing there?" Haley demanded.

"Maybe *we* should be asking *you* the same question," Irene said, finally noticing her. Haley blushed.

"Dude, did you just see that volley! It was sick!" Chopper enthused, still transfixed by Coco De Clerq.

"Trust me, fellows, she's not *really* serious about this," Spencer said loud enough for Coco to hear. "Since when is Coco De Clerq *serious* about *anything*?" And with that, he turned and walked away.

Coco, meanwhile, never missed a stroke.

"Dude, why you gotta harsh on her like that?" Chopper called after Spencer, puffing out his chest. "Don't hate the playa, hate the game!" he yelled.

"Chopper, man," Shaun said, throwing an arm around him, "that's deep."

• • •

Who would ever have thought that Coco De Clerq would be reduced to grunting in the parking lot in front of the freaks and geeks she used to torment? Do you think she's serious about her latest athletic pursuit? Or is she just hoping her string of wins on the court will eventually win back Spencer's affections?

What about Devon? Will Haley ever be willing to put up with his aloof ways, moody artistic tendencies and near-constant family struggles? Or is that package a gift that keeps on taking?

To stick with the artistically gifted circus act and catch up with Devon at JACK'S, turn to page 47. Alternatively, if you think Coco's newfound interest in tennis has awakened Haley's competitive nature, skip to IN THE SWING on page 40.

Six months ago, no one would have thought that Coco would be an outcast and Irene would have a boyfriend, least of all Haley. The good thing about turning tables: there's always a new place to sit.

Beware the mystery meat.

Haley had decided to give Sasha and Johnny the benefit of the doubt. *They must have some explanation for why they've been MIA since we got back from Paris,* she thought, heading to the cafeteria later that day to meet up with her friends.

Reese Highland, however, was another story. Haley was holding him to a *much* higher standard. After all, he had made out with her in Paris, which to Haley meant they were as good as dating. And yet she hadn't heard from him once since they had touched down at Newark airport.

What if Paris was just a fling? she suddenly wondered, momentarily panicking before straightening her posture and entering the lunchroom. *I'll just have to show him what he's missing.*

Haley spotted Sasha and Cecily Watson at their usual table. The boys, it seemed, either weren't there yet or were waiting in line to buy lunch. It was astounding how much cafeteria food they could eat. And today's hot lunch was meat loaf. Haley shuddered.

"Wasn't that just the most amazing trip?" Cecily was saying to Sasha as Haley walked up.

"Johnny and I loved the canal Saint-Martin," said Sasha. "Now I know why it took my mom so long to come back to boring old Hillsdale."

Haley cleared her throat and forced a smile.

"Hey," the girls said in unison.

Haley tried to read the meaning behind their greetings—their body language, their furtive glances at one another. Finally, after several minutes of silence, Cecily said, "Why are you acting so weird?"

"Um, why are *you* acting so weird?" Haley asked in return.

"Come on, Haley," said Sasha. "Ever since we got back from Paris, you've been *odd*. And paranoid."

"I thought maybe after seven days of constant togetherness, you guys were sick of me," Haley said, plopping down in a chair. "How come you didn't return my calls over the weekend?"

"Um, I did try calling you back," said Cecily. "Twice. But all I got was a bunch of static."

Haley blushed. "Guess reception was pretty bad up at my grandmother's farm."

"Awwww, you really thought we were ignoring you?" Sasha teased. "Hales, you're the greatest. We'd never dump you. Unless you started hanging out with Coco."

Before Haley could respond, a pair of warm hands covered her eyes. She'd have known those palms anywhere, just by the scent of the soap. "Reese?" Haley asked, spinning around in her chair. And there he was, her adorable neighbor, with his dark, mussed hair, tan skin and green eyes. Reese flashed her that killer Highland grin, then leaned down and gave her a peck on the lips.

Paris was definitely not a fling, Haley thought, trying her hardest to stay mad at him.

"Sorry I disappeared on you this weekend," he said before Haley had a chance to scold him. "I tried calling you back on Saturday but couldn't get through. And you know, track and field starts this week. I've been running my legs off every moment I'm not eating or sleeping."

"Ugh, don't remind me. My quads are so not ready for those hurdle drills," Cecily said.

Haley felt awash with relief. And she silently vowed not to let herself get so worked up again.

"Let me just establish my times, and I'm all yours," Reese added, and grabbed a handful of carrot sticks and whole wheat crackers from Sasha's lunch bag.

Haley turned to Cecily. "So you're going out for the track team too?" she asked.

"Somebody's got to make sure Drew moves his lazy bones around that field."

"Me three," said Sasha. "That sprint work does wonders for my soccer game. You should think about joining us, Haley."

"Yeah, we need to get you back in fighting Hawks shape," said Reese, pinching Haley's puny bicep and then pinching off a piece of her turkey and avocado on seven-grain bread.

"I'll . . . um, think about it," Haley replied, watching Reese devour half of her lunch.

"Tryouts start this afternoon," Cecily advised as Reese sneaked one of her cookies. "Boy, go buy yourself some food!"

Reese laughed. "Be right back," he said, hopping up from the table, kissing Haley on the top of the head and dashing over to cut in line with Drew Napolitano and Johnny Lane.

"That guy is a horse," said Cecily. "I'll bet he eats

his body weight three times a week. . . . But," she added, turning to Haley, "he sure seems into you."

"You think so?" Haley replied, reveling in her new status as Reese Highland's girlfriend. Within minutes, the boys were plopping down at the table, carrying lunch trays piled high with meaty subs, chef's salads, caffeinated sodas and various snacks.

"Boys will be pigs," Cecily said, holding out the sides of her shirt to indicate that they were bound to balloon out if they didn't watch it.

"How can you eat that stuff?" Haley asked, pointing to the mystery meat slice on Reese's tray.

"When I'm this hungry, I'll eat anything," he said.

"Even Fanny Pincus's meat loaf," Drew added.

"Hey, Sash, don't forget—practice starts an hour earlier as of tonight," Johnny reminded her. "We've got a lot of set work to rehearse before the Battle of the Bands."

"Yeah, about that . . . ," Sasha began tentatively. "I've got track until six."

Johnny looked surprised and maybe a little annoyed. "So you're really gonna do both?"

Sasha nodded, silently continuing to eat her lunch. Johnny clenched his jaw. *Well, this is awkward,* Haley thought, turning away momentarily to give them some space. Across the cafeteria, she spotted Annie and Dave, feet up, sunglasses on, faces totally relaxed.

Are they . . . napping? Haley wondered, then watched as Whitney Klein approached them with her sack lunch. Whitney said something, motioning to the chair where Dave's feet were propped. Dave twitched a little and rolled over. Whitney, careful not to disturb him, pulled up another chair, sat down, and began to self-consciously nibble her food.

"Yo, check out Witless Klein eating with Head-strong and Putzger," Drew said, staring in the trio's direction.

"What is Whitney doing having lunch with Annie and Dave?" Sasha asked.

"And shouldn't those two be working on the yearbook?" Cecily added, nodding at Annie and Dave. "It's due at the printer in two weeks, and I've heard they are *way* behind."

Strange things were certainly afoot in Hillsdale. *Annie and Dave slacking off and ignoring a deadline? Whitney eating in public without Coco De Clerq? What is going on?* Haley wondered, relieved to be ensconced in her happy little friend bubble. Although with tension building between Sasha and Johnny, how long could their charmed existence last?

● ● ●

Haley certainly gave in to Reese Highland's charms quickly, but then who wouldn't melt at that smile? Do you think she should've taken a harder line with him? Is Reese's disappearing act something for her to be

concerned about? What about his habit of taking things without asking? Is Reese secretly kind of a jerk? Or will he prove to be the perfect boyfriend? And will Haley have to join the track team to keep him?

To send Haley to try out for TRACK AND FIELD with the others, turn to page 51. If you think the Hillsdale universe is completely out of whack and want to restore some order, take the reins of the yearbook from newly anointed slackers Annie and Dave on page 59 (POLL POSITION). Alternatively, find out where Coco De Clerq's been hiding out in IN THE SWING on page 40. Or send Haley home to spend some time with her family and consider her options on page 70 (GOOD HAIR DAY).

Whatever Reese's faults, he's still the cutest boy in school. Does Haley have the willpower to walk away?

RULE BY COMMITTEE

Mob rule is never pretty.

Haley decided to give Annie and Dave the benefit of the doubt. She figured there must be some explanation for why, after they had spent spring break together in Spain, her traveling companions were practically ignoring her. And that included her is-he-or-isn't-he boyfriend, Sebastian Bodega, whom Haley hadn't heard from since they'd gone their separate ways at Newark airport.

Haley agreed to meet Annie and Dave that afternoon at their yearbook committee meeting, hoping to get some answers. But when she arrived, Annie was sitting at Ms. Lipsky's desk with her feet up, casually flipping through a magazine. *"Hola, mucha-cha. Qué pasa?"* she asked Haley. Annie was drinking a glass of iced lemonade and cooling herself with an accordion fan.

"You asked *me* to swing by," Haley said incredulously.

Annie shrugged. "Whatever."

"Aren't you supposed to be editing something?" Haley added, glancing over Annie's shoulder at the untouched pile of work on Ms. Lipsky's desk.

"Ah, this yearbook stuff is a cakewalk," said Annie, getting up from her chair and strolling around the room. "The thing practically writes itself." She motioned to a huddle of freshmen who were haphazardly laying out pages and making photo selections. The group didn't seem to have the slightest clue what they were doing.

Hannah Moss, the pygmy-sized genius from Haley and Annie's Spanish class, held up a stunning photo of Coco De Clerq and Whitney Klein. "This one okay for an opener?" Hannah asked Annie.

"Sure," Annie replied, shooing her away.

Haley was shocked. The whole reason Annie had worked so hard to become the youngest yearbook editor ever in Hillsdale High history was so she could get back at Coco and Whitney for all those times they had tortured her. The plan was to use horrendously bad photos of them in the *Talon,* thus rewriting history and rendering their popularity a dim memory. Now here she was letting Hannah include the most gorgeous photo of Coco and Whitney ever? What was going on?

"All right, kids, enough work," Annie commanded, giving another blasé wave of her hand. "It's siesta time." She lay down on a bench next to a row of windows, closed her eyes and resumed fanning herself.

"Annie, the yearbook proof is due in, like, two weeks," Haley exclaimed, horrified at her friend's behavior.

"Who cares?" Annie replied. "Do you know I just figured out that I could get Cs on all my finals and still make As for the year? Kinda makes a girl want to forget about schoolwork and stop and smell the roses for a change." With that, Annie plucked a rosebud from a bouquet on Ms. Lipsky's desk and inhaled deeply, then lay back down. "Now, that's more like it."

"Hey, I had fun in Seville too," Haley said. "But come on—"

Annie sighed. "Gosh, I wish we were back there right now, sitting under the stars on Sebastian's patio."

"Me . . . too . . . ," Dave Metzger chimed in from the back of the room, where he was sitting at a computer screen, staring at a slide show of images from their trip instead of making photo selections for the yearbook.

"Guys, snap out of it!" Haley said, her frustration increasing. "You can't just shirk your responsibilities. There's serious work to do."

"Oh, can't we?" Annie asked, settling deeper into her relaxed state.

"Fine. Hannah, what else are you working on over there?" Haley demanded, taking matters into her own hands.

"Um, it's a page on senioritis," Hannah said, proudly holding up her work.

Haley examined the messy collage and gasped. "But half of those people aren't even in the senior class!

"And you, over there, with the braids," Haley added, pointing to a girl handling the junior-class portraits pages. "Let me see that," Haley said, picking up a proof sheet. "Are you kidding me? All the names are off!"

"Huh?" the girl asked innocently.

"Does *he* look like an Angela to you?" Haley demanded.

"Oh yeah, I thought that seemed a little weird," the girl confided.

"And what are *you* staring at?" Haley barked, looking over at the latest addition to the yearbook committee, Irene Chen, who had been appointed to illustrate the *Talon* cover.

Irene glowered behind her silky black hair with its yellow streaks. "Absolutely nothing," Irene said, then added under her breath, "I guess *someone* had to fill the power vacuum."

"Well, *someone* has to make sure we actually have a yearbook this year," Haley said, looking down at the drawing Irene was laboring away at. It was a picture of a guitar, with members of the Hedon and Rubber Dynamite clustered on either side, and a Battle of the Bands banner at the top. "*That* certainly doesn't look like *Talon* cover art!"

Irene smirked. "I can't draw the cover until the committee decides on a theme," she retorted, sitting back in her chair and folding her arms across her chest.

"You mean to tell me you people never settled on a *theme*?" Haley roared, her gaze searching the room. "What have you been *doing* for the past few weeks?"

"Well, Annie could never make up her mind," Hannah offered. "And you've seen what she's like since she came back from spring break."

Haley rolled up her sleeves. "Okay, people, we've got tons of work to do, and precious little time to do it in," she said, picking up a box of unsorted class portraits. "You, girl with the braids, pull all the *Talon* yearbooks from the past three years so we can accurately ID any upperclassmen we don't personally know, and also get me class lists from all the homeroom teachers.

"Irene, here's our theme: 'Hawk Eye.' Now get started on that image. I want to see something by tomorrow, end of day.

"Hannah, see if you can find any spare bodies who want to help. We're going to need all the manpower we can get."

Haley then began sifting through pages in a COMPLETED folder to check for errors, when something—or rather, someone—caught her eye. Through the open window, she saw Sebastian Bodega smiling, throwing his head back in laughter and of course looking incredibly hot. *Finally,* she thought. *It's about time he came and found me.*

Then Haley spotted his companion. It was a girl. A very pretty girl with long dark hair, endless legs and smooth olive skin, dressed in a red miniskirt and tan espadrilles. "Who is that?" Haley blurted out suspiciously.

Annie glanced at the couple through the window. "Oh, that's just Mia, Sebastian's old girlfriend from Spain," she said nonchalantly. "Didn't he tell you about her? She's a model or something. I think she had some go-sees in New York last week, so she came out to Hillsdale this weekend for a visit. She's staying with the Shopes."

Haley's blood chilled. *So that's why I haven't heard from Sebastian since we came back from our trip! His supermodel ex-girlfriend is in town! They're probably sleeping in the same bed at the Shopes'!* Haley sat down and forcefully began flipping through a box of Hillsdale Hawks sports photos, trying to disguise her shock and dismay. *You'd think he would have had the decency to tell me she was coming into town, so I wouldn't have to hear it from Annie, of all people. I could've handled that. Did he think I couldn't handle that? I am an understanding girl!*

Haley was so hurt and angry, she almost didn't notice the stack of pictures of her adorable neighbor, Reese Highland—on the soccer field, shooting layups on the basketball court—in her hands. Almost.

Haley looked down. In every photo, Reese was in some form of a blue and gold Hawks uniform, and inevitably it showcased his chiseled biceps, rock-hard quads and well-defined calves. A thought occurred to her. *Well, maybe I'm just too busy to see Sebastian now,* she thought, studying the images. *After all, he's not the only boy at Hillsdale High.*

How right she was. Haley felt a tap on her shoulder. She looked up to find her classmate, the ultra-cute photographer Devon McKnight.

"Um, hi," Haley said awkwardly, returning the photos of Reese to the stack. She felt her face flush. "Are you here to join the yearbook committee? We certainly need the help."

"Not really," Devon explained. "A couple of weeks ago, Annie asked me to do some reshoots of the 'pictorially challenged' members of the sophomore class. She said you might want your portrait redone?"

Haley suddenly remembered that her yearbook photo had turned out, well, less than flattering. At the time, Annie had suggested Haley bring in her own head shot instead. But when Haley had looked through her recent photos, she couldn't find *anything* that would work. Haley was, after all, a person who had always been much more comfortable behind the camera than in front of it. In all the excitement over the trip to Spain, she'd forgotten about the photo entirely, but apparently that was the one yearbook duty Annie hadn't overlooked.

Haley looked over at Annie, who gave her a lazy wink and a nod.

"Actually, you were the only person Annie mentioned as being a 'critical' case," Devon continued. He pulled out a stack of proofs Annie had given him and flipped to the page showing Haley. Her eyes were at half-mast, her lip was curled up on one side, all Elvis-like, and it looked as if she had spilled something on her shirt.

"Whoa." Haley frowned. "That's heinous. We definitely don't want that in the yearbook."

"Don't take it personally," Devon said, trying to make her feel better. "It's just those school photographer hacks. They could screw up a model's face." Haley winced, recalling the image of Sebastian outside with his ex. *I bet they couldn't screw up Mia's face,* she thought. "You're such a pretty girl, all someone really has to do is point and shoot," Devon added, salvaging his point. Haley gave him a half smile. "So, this time tomorrow? We'll snap a few quick portraits?"

"Sure." Haley nodded, trying to act unimpressed as he threw his skateboard down, waved goodbye and sailed off through the empty hall.

● ● ●

Well, that was certainly a shocker. Do you think Sebastian is cheating on Haley? Can she compete with a Spanish supermodel? And was Sebastian's affection in Seville just an act?

To CONFRONT SEBASTIAN about hosting his ex-girlfriend at the Shopes', turn to page 66. If you think Haley should forget Sebastian and stick with the yearbook committee to make sure the *Talon* actually makes it to the presses this year, go to POLL POSITION on page 59. If you're more interested in having Devon retake Haley's portrait and finding out if there are any flashes between them, turn to RESHOOTS WITH DEVON on page 113. Finally, see what Reese Highland's been up to in TRACK AND FIELD on page 51.

High school boyfriends are like second helpings. They can be fun to indulge in, but ultimately they're expendable.

**When a body is in motion
and that body belongs to
Coco De Clerq, get the
heck out of her way.**

"Nice one!" Chopper yelled after Coco De Clerq aced another serve. Haley walked toward the in-progess practice session on the tennis courts, still amazed that Coco had emerged as such a talented competitor. Then again, given Coco's fierceness in the halls of Hillsdale High, it wasn't exactly a surprise to see her dismantle opponents on the court.

Haley sat down in the bleachers, not far from where Chopper was planted. He saw her and moved back two rows to join her. "Isn't that two-handed thing she does with the racket just the most beautiful thing you've ever seen?" he asked.

"Uh, you mean her backhand?" Haley asked. "Yeah, it's pretty fierce."

"And the way she grunts a little on her follow-through, and then spits . . ." Chopper bit his lip and clutched his chest. "I could marry that girl."

"Good luck," Haley warned. Whitney Klein approached, offering a much-needed alternative to Chopper's play-by-play. Haley called her over.

"Hey," said Whitney, eyeing Chopper for a moment before holding her purse a little tighter. She pulled Haley a few seats down. "We have got to talk about this tennis thing," Whitney began in a whisper. "Coco has gone completely over the edge. It's impossible to hang out with her anymore. You know she's stopped returning my calls? We've spoken every day since we were old enough to have phone lines, which is since we were old enough to talk. And now just because her coach is telling her to focus, she can't take my calls?"

At that moment, Haley realized that Whitney Klein only knew how to be a sidekick. At every stage of her life, she had been Coco De Clerq's second-in-command, her aide-de-camp. Now that Coco's reign over the sophomore class was crumbling, Whitney could no longer play follow the leader. There were no more public appearances for the Coquettes to make. No inferiors to torture. No wannabes to snub.

Her lifelong position as Coco's number-one wingbabe had been eliminated. Haley felt genuinely sorry for her.

"Playing a varsity sport is a really time-consuming commitment," she reminded Whitney. "But it's probably good for Coco, don't you think? She's finally putting all those years of country club lessons to use."

"Well, I happen to think it's weird to play a sport," Whitney said, frowning. "I would *never* run voluntarily. Haven't you seen what it can do to your quads? Sasha Lewis and Cecily Watson are totally going to beef up now that they're joining the track team."

"They're *what*?" Haley asked, following Whitney's gaze to the field, where Cecily, Sasha and Haley's hot neighbor, Reese Highland, were all stretching. Meanwhile, Shaun Willkommen bounded onto the green, wearing a vintage seventies gold tracksuit and blue sweatbands and belting out "We Are the Champions."

Haley felt a pang of jealousy, partly because Sasha and Cecily would be on a team together and partly because they would be spending so much time with Reese.

"So, Haley," Whitney pried, seeing where Haley's attention had drifted. "What's with you and Natural Highland these days?"

Not much, unfortunately, Haley felt like saying,

but she knew better than to confide in a chatterbox like Whitney. She also knew that she wouldn't even have to bother changing the subject. It was widely known that Whitney had the worst case of ADD in Bergen County.

"Oh my God!" Whitney blurted out, practically tugging on Haley's arm. "Do you know those geeks from Spanish class, Annie Armstrong and Dave Metzger? Well, they totally got busy over spring break in Spain. Isn't that, like, the grossest thing you've ever heard?"

"I don't know if *geek* is necessarily the right word anymore," Haley said, motioning to Annie and Dave as they breezed across the parking lot. Annie was in dark tortoiseshell sunglasses and a long flowing goddess dress, clearly something she picked up on her trip to Spain, while Dave had on jeans, a white T-shirt and a navy blue blazer. They had about a dozen freshmen trailing after them, hanging on their every word, but Annie and Dave looked as though they couldn't have cared less.

Guess someone's blowing off a yearbook committee meeting, Haley guessed, remembering that Annie was supposed to be editing the *Talon* this year.

"What is going *on*?" Whitney said, gritting her teeth. "The whole world's upside down. Do you know, my mom is thinking about *moving in* with Sasha's dad? I mean, they just started dating, and now they're shacking up? And I can't even escape to my dad's house because he's still off who-knows-where with Trish." Whitney looked over at Haley and batted her eyes. "Maybe I can come stay with you, Haley? I mean, I'd much rather be sisters with you than that *jock* Sasha Lewis."

Haley cringed. She could only imagine what life with Whitney 24–7 would be like, though she somehow knew it would involve at least two hair dryers and a lot of eye shadow.

"That's my girl!" Chopper yelled as Coco smashed a forehand across the net. Haley clapped politely, glancing over her shoulder again. She had hoped that Reese might have noticed her sitting up there in the bleachers, but he had already stopped stretching and walked off toward the field where the rest of the track team was assembled. She wondered if there was any girl on earth who could truly turn his head.

"Forty–love," the tennis coach called out, announcing the score.

"What's love got to do with it?" pondered Whitney, utterly confused. "Sometimes I think umpires just make up this stuff as they go along. No one could ever remember all these little rules, much less that lingo. What's a 'let'? And how do you 'volley'? Isn't that for volleyball?"

At that moment, Coco aced another serve to win the game.

"Thank goodness," Whitney said, standing up. "I don't think I could take another second of this." But then Coco and her teammate just switched sides of the court, and Coco took her position to receive. "Are you kidding me? They're playing *again*?" Whitney whined.

"It's called a set," said Haley. "They play until someone wins six games."

"*Six!* I really have got to find something better to do with my afternoons." Whitney sighed.

No kidding, Haley thought. Though she couldn't help feeling the same way.

• • •

Even if Coco's no longer Hillsdale's teen queen, her rule over Bergen County's tennis courts has just begun. But where does that leave poor Whitney? Is it Miss Klein's turn to find a hobby? And what, if anything, would she be good at?

Reese is once again demonstrating athletic prowess on a field. But will he ever love a girl the way he loves his running shoes and soccer balls?

To start tracking Reese's every move after school, send Haley to try out for TRACK AND FIELD on page 51. If you think playing a sport to be closer to a boy is a bad move and could thwart any love connection with Reese, stick with the girls formerly known as populettes and see if Whitney has an original bone in her body in

MATCH POINT on page 74. Finally, have Haley rescue the yearbook from newfound slackers Annie and Dave in POLL POSITION on page 59, and make sure the *Talon* actually goes to press.

High school is known for its drama. But what if . . . there were no yearbook to take it all down?

Life on the run
often requires a disguise.

"My new physique just *screams* for Lycra," Shaun announced while flipping through a rack of old tracksuits at Jack's Vintage Clothing in Hillsdale. He had just selected a royal blue one with white stripes and placed it in his "keepers" pile. "This'll do nicely. I dropped me another dress size just this week."

Haley noticed that Shaun *did* seem to be looking trimmer, though for Shaun, that still meant an ample double chin and love handles that wrapped around to a sizeable gut.

Irene knelt down on the floor next to Haley and started rummaging through a black plastic bag of recently donated clothes. "Hold your starter pistols—*this* is it," she said, fetching out a gold lamé jumpsuit that had clearly belonged to a big-boned woman in the eighties.

"Cha-ching, bada-bing, the holy grail of workout wear," said Shaun. "And ye shall be my competitive ensemble."

"Great price, too," Devon McKnight said, smirking. Haley knew what that meant. Anything new to the store that hadn't been marked yet was basically fair game. You could name your price. Devon worked at Jack's after school to make extra money, which made going there to shop that much more fun.

"Oh, Haley," Devon added, "I found something in the back I thought you might like."

Haley's eyes widened as he handed her something else that was gold and shiny. "They're incredible," she said, examining the sparkly green-gem-studded earrings.

"Could be emeralds, but hey, what do I know," Devon said. "I'm sure we get estate jewels in here all the time that sell for three bucks."

"Maybe you should look into getting gemologist certification," Irene recommended. "I bet we could make a fortune."

"Ba-da-bum . . . ba-da-bum . . . ," Shaun growled, bursting out of the dressing room in a blaze of gold, humming the theme song to *Rocky* and chasing Irene around the store, throwing shadow punches.

Devon, meanwhile, had to take care of some real customers, so while Shaun and Irene tussled, Haley checked her phone for messages. She had two texts in her in-box. The first was from, of all people, Coco De Clerq:

Haley . . . My coach wants someone to film my matches so that we can analyze my stroke. Interested? Pays $100 per game . . . C.

Haley was intrigued. *Talk about a gold mine,* she thought, scrolling down to the second text. This one was from Sasha Lewis:

Haleykins, we so desperately need you on the track team. Cecily and I are dying for company, and the rest of the girls' team is shall we say talent poor this season. Why don't you come try out? Reese has been asking about you . . . Sash.

Haley thought back to the first day of the school year, when Coco and Sasha were best friends and, along with Whitney Klein, were idolized by the rest of their classmates. Now here were Coco and Sasha, both texting *her,* Haley Miller. Both in need of her help. Haley knew she shouldn't revel in the moment, but it was kind of hard not to enjoy it at least a little. She decided she would take the night to think over both requests and give her answers in the morning. The two former populettes could wait.

Haley seems very much in demand these days. Sasha and Coco need her help. Reese is asking about her. And Devon just presented her with a pair of bejeweled earrings. If Haley does decide to take Coco up on her offer of a hundred dollars a game, will Devon stick around to help her spend the money? Alternatively, should Haley stop rooting for Shaun and join the track team?

To have Haley witness Shaun's athletic debut with Irene and Devon, go to page 80 (TRACKSIDE SEATS). If you think Haley should join the team herself, turn to page 51 (TRACK AND FIELD).

Coco seems to be acting differently now that she's in a tennis league of her own. Find out if she's really on the upswing on page 74, MATCH POINT. Finally, if you think Haley should extend her time-out to assess her options, send her home to spend time with her family on page 70 (GOOD HAIR DAY).

Some people are made for the sidelines. Others won't be satisfied until they're in the racing lanes—or at the net—themselves. It's up to you to figure out where to put Haley: in the cheering section or in the middle of all the action.

TRACK AND FIELD

It's much easier to run when you've got something to chase.

On the second day of track and field tryouts, Haley ran into Cecily Watson and Sasha Lewis in the Hawks' gold and blue locker room. "Well, look who decided to join us," said Cecily, teasing Haley as she laced up her track shoes before practice. "You sure you're ready for gauntlet runs and time trials, Miller?"

Haley pulled her hair back into a high ponytail and said confidently, "Not only am I ready, Watson, but I think I can take you."

"Hel-lo!" said Sasha. "Forget gauntlet runs. She just threw the gauntlet *down*."

"*That* skinny little thing? My *breakfast* is bigger than her," Cecily said, furrowing her brow and circling Haley like a drill sergeant examining a cadet. "High knees!" Cecily suddenly commanded. Haley looked at her for a second, then began running furiously in place, lifting her knees up to almost touch her chest. "Push-ups!" Cecily yelled next. Haley dropped to the floor and gave her five. "Now go pants Reese Highland!" Cecily bellowed. Haley jumped up to obey the command, then realized what Cecily had just said. She smirked as Sasha and Cecily collapsed in laughter.

"She was halfway to the field!" Sasha giggled.

"That girl knows how to take orders!" Cecily said, holding her sides.

In the middle of their fun, a very businesslike Coco De Clerq marched into the locker room, carrying her tennis racket along with a summery green tote emblazoned with her country club's logo. She didn't even bother to say hello but went straight to her locker to drop off her things.

"Hi, Coco," Sasha said, attempting to break the ice queen. Her greeting was met with stony silence. "Hello?" Sasha added, pressing Coco for a response. "Can't you even say hi to someone you've known your entire life?"

Still nothing.

"Come on, let's go," said Cecily, tugging on Sasha's arm. "Let that spider get caught in her own web. Haley, you coming?"

Haley smiled in Coco's general direction on her way out of the locker room, but Coco was still avoiding eye contact. She methodically hung up her bag and took out a brush, giving each side seven strokes before pulling her dark locks back into a ponytail.

Haley wondered just what it was that kept Coco so aloof: haughtiness, pride and a sense of entitlement? Or was she so focused on tennis that everything else, including friends, had ceased to matter? Had she really been wounded by her sudden dethronement at Hillsdale High? And did she have no other choice now but to keep all her feelings bottled up? It was a mystery wrapped in an enigma.

Out on the field, Reese Highland broke into a grin and started clapping as Haley walked over to join the team. "Glad you could make it, Miller," he said. Coach Tygert too seemed happy to have another able body on the field, though evidently, he didn't need it.

"Girls' times in the four-hundred-meter dash have already exceeded the fastest in Hillsdale High history," he reported. "If Cecily Watson's time yesterday had been clocked officially during a meet, a 1999 school record would've been obliterated."

"You still think you can take me, Miller?" Cecily teased.

"Bring it," Haley whispered back.

"Now, I know some of you here might be new to track," Coach Tygert continued, looking directly at Haley. "For those of you wondering where you're going to fit in—"

Before Coach Tygert could finish his thought, Irene Chen appeared in the stands and lifted a boom box high over her head. She hit a switch and "Eye of the Tiger" began blasting across the field. A few seconds later, a blur of blue and gold came bursting out of the locker room.

"Isn't that . . . Shaun?" Haley gasped, watching their still-somewhat-tubby classmate run circles around the team. He was dressed in a vintage blue poly-blend tracksuit, accented with gold sweatbands on his wrists and forehead.

"As I was saying," Coach Tygert continued, undeterred. "Track and field is not about fitting in. We encourage you all to be different, to figure out what your strengths—and weaknesses—are. And then we challenge you to better yourself, better your form, better your times."

"Yeehaw, coach, I'm having a grand ol' time right now," said Shaun, strutting slalom style around the hurdles.

"I'll just bet you are, Shaun," Coach Tygert replied. "Now, we have a slew of top returning distance runners. And two of our best hurdlers are back: Cecily Watson and Reese Highland. As for high jumpers, shot-putters, discus throwers, triple and long jumpers—the field, as they say, is wide open. And we will need to find someone to replace state champ Kendra Abrams on girls' relay."

"Go, Haley!" Sasha yelled.

"Yay Miller!" Reese chimed in. Haley blushed.

"Pssst." Haley heard an out-of-breath whisper from a few paces away. She turned to see Shaun, his face red. He kept jerking his head slightly, as if to motion her over, and pointing to his pocket.

Like I want to see what's in there, Haley thought.

"Hay-wey," Shaun said out of the side of his mouth. His ventriloquist act was fooling no one, though, and Coach Tygert looked over at the two of them with a raised eyebrow.

Haley decided she'd better see what Shaun wanted before he got them both into trouble. As casually as possible, she sidestepped to join him and glanced down at the item that was now in his left hand. It was . . . a proof of Haley's school yearbook picture. And it was her worst one yet. Her eyes were at half-mast, her lip was curled up, all Elvis-like, and she seemed to have splattered some breakfast cereal on her top that morning. Haley was horrified. She froze, unsure of what he intended to do with the evidence.

I bet he weaseled it out of the yearbook committee, she thought, narrowing her eyes at Shaun. *I wonder how many people have seen it.* "What are you after, Willkommen?" Haley quietly demanded.

"Who, me?" Shaun said innocently, galloping over to the other side of the huddle. He inched closer and closer to Reese Highland, all the while looking back over his shoulder to gauge Haley's increasingly horrified expression. Each step he took toward Reese pushed Haley just a wee bit closer to her breaking point. Just as Shaun was about to tap her cute neighbor on the shoulder and presumably show him Haley's embarrassing school portrait, she dashed over to stop him.

Shaun broke away from the group and took off, running as fast as he could down the track. As he picked up speed and sprinted 50, 100, 150 meters, Haley heard the theme from *Chariots of Fire* blasting out of Irene's boom box. That only made her angrier. *She must be in on this,* Haley thought, gaining on Shaun until she was finally able to grab him by his tracksuit collar.

"Gotcha," Haley said, pulling him to a halt and ripping his jacket off in the process. Haley confiscated the school picture and tore it to shreds before rejoining the group.

"I won't even ask what that was about," said Coach Tygert as she approached, "but not a bad time, Miller. Looks like we might have just found the missing link for the girls' relay team. Way to turn on the gas."

The wheezing Shaun heard that and, of course, began making disgusting fart noises by pressing his palms against his mouth and blowing.

"Haley," Coach Tygert said, ignoring Shaun's antics, "pair up with Cecily and Sasha for drills."

As Haley readied herself for the next run, she couldn't help noticing Irene gawking and smirking at her from atop the chain-link fence. *Yep,* thought Haley, *she is most definitely in on it.* Haley began plotting her revenge.

Reese surprised her first, though, sneaking up on her and whispering in her ear, "Maybe we should have Shaun wave that thing around before every one of your races. That was like watching a rabbit at a greyhound track. Now I know who I want for a partner in the three-legged race on field day."

Haley laughed it off, but she was secretly worried. If she didn't figure out a way to have her photo retaken, and quick, that awful proof might end up being published in the actual yearbook. And then everyone would see it, including Reese.

The only thing that gave her a moment's solace was a possibly fictitious rumor about Annie Armstrong. Evidently, Annie was slacking off on her yearbook editor duties, and the *Talon* wasn't expected to make it to the presses on time. According to several people on the yearbook committee, there might not even be a *Talon* this year.

That would certainly solve a lot of problems, Haley thought, giving her quads one last stretch. As she made her way to the starting line for the first time trial, she wondered if she should indeed chance it.

● ● ●

Well, that was certainly close. Reese nearly saw Haley in her worst possible state. But what exactly do you think he would have done if he had glimpsed Haley's bad picture? Teased her lovingly? Or run the other way? Do yearbook photos even matter to Reese? And should they matter to Haley?

If you think there's nothing more humiliating than a really awful yearbook portrait and you want Haley to do something about it pronto, turn to page 113 (RESHOOTS WITH DEVON).

If you think spending time with Reese Highland is far more important than some silly picture, go to page 86 (FIELD DAY).

To have Haley check up on Coco De Clerq before her next practice at the local COUNTRY CLUB, turn to page 105.

Anyone who ever said "Beauty is only skin deep" never took a bad yearbook picture. Surely, if the photo does run, Haley can look forward to several months—make that a full year—of torture from the lips of her classmates. But is it worth putting her life on hold to fix?

POLL POSITION

**No one cares for polls,
except for politicians.**

Haley gave Ms. Frick's desk a good thwack with a wooden yardstick, then cleared her throat loudly, calling the *Talon* yearbook committee meeting to order. "Take your seats, Talonites," she said, a smile creeping across her face. Having officially taken over for Annie Armstrong as committee chair, Haley found she was beginning to enjoy the newfound power and privilege of her job. At least it kept her from thinking about superhot Spanish exchange student Sebastian Bodega and the fact that he had recently reunited with his supermodel ex-girlfriend, Mia Delgado.

"Now for our first order of business," Haley commanded. Despite the fact Haley had never been in charge of a school activity group before, much less taken on something as crucial as yearbook production, she exuded confidence—in herself, in the committee, in their ability to get the *Talon* ready before its fast-approaching deadline—which was almost as good as hard experience. As far as Haley was concerned, the departing senior class would not be without a final memento of their public education experience. Not on her watch. And by sheer force of will, she was about to pull it off.

Annie Armstrong, on the other hand, had literally taken a backseat on the project. Annie was currently in the last row of desks with her constant companion, Dave Metzger, whispering in his ear, oblivious to the progress Haley had made over the past few days.

"Ahem." Haley cleared her throat for a second time.

Annie paused, looked up indifferently and said, "Come on, Haley. It's only a yearbook."

Haley couldn't believe her ears. A month ago, Annie "Headstrong" would have kicked someone off the committee for uttering such heresy.

"Well, for those who are interested in fulfilling their responsibilities as members of this committee, I am pleased to announce that Irene has nearly finished our cover," Haley said, holding up the sketch Irene Chen had been furiously working on—an extreme closeup on a predatory bird's eye and beak. "This is perfect for our theme, 'Hawk Eye.' Thank you, Irene." Irene seemed surprised to receive the compliment.

"Hannah, good progress on your senioritis page," Haley said, looking over Hannah's shoulder at the neatly reconstructed collage, which now showed just the eyes of various Hillsdale High students. "Even if all those people aren't actually seniors, it will be impossible to tell. And besides, people will have fun guessing."

Haley next saw that a group of kids assigned to proofread the names next to all the class photos had nearly completed their task. *Getting close,* she thought, feeling satisfied.

"I guess we'll get started on tallying up the nominations for the class polls," she said loudly, hoping to catch Annie's attention this time. But as Haley returned to her seat at Ms. Lipsky's desk and picked up the box of early poll sheets, she saw that Annie and Dave were still canoodling at the back of the room. For the next two hours, Haley and her minions counted and recounted the nominations for every class poll category, from Most Likely to Succeed to Class Clown, Most Attractive to Teacher's Pet, for the freshmen through the seniors.

"Um, Haley," Hannah said, approaching Haley at her desk. Hannah was responsible for counting the sophomore-class ballots.

"Yes, Hannah?" Haley asked, somewhat annoyed by the interruption.

"I just thought you should know. It looks like you were nominated for Best All Around."

While it was a given that people like Sasha Lewis and Cecily Watson would be nominated for that most coveted of categories, Haley was shocked to discover that she, Haley Miller, had been included. "Let me see those," she said, examining the nominating forms. Sure enough, more than four dozen sophomores had written her name down. Not nearly as many votes as Sasha and Cecily had gotten, but still enough to get her name on the final ballot. *Holy smokes,* Haley thought, unsure of what this meant. *Could I be approaching the popularity level of Sasha and Cecily? Or is someone just playing a sick joke on me?*

"Thank you, Hannah" was all Haley said before diving back into her work. Much as she would have liked to analyze her nomination and its implications, she simply didn't have time.

At six o'clock, when she finally looked up again, Haley discovered that she and Irene Chen were the only two yearbook committee members left in the room. Annie and Dave had long since snuck out, and theirs had evidently triggered a series of departures.

Now, Gunter, the night watchman, was flipping off the lights in the adjoining classrooms and hall one by one.

"I think it's time for me to go," Irene said sleepily, packing up her art supplies. "I've still got to go relieve the hostess at the Dynasty for the late shift."

Haley studied Irene intently. "I'm sorry I ever called you a slacker," she said.

"You didn't," Irene replied.

"Well, not to your face, anyway," Haley added, blushing. "I should probably get out of here too," she said, gathering up her belongings. The last thing Haley wanted was to be left alone in a darkened classroom. Gunter, who was partially blind, and deaf in one ear, was famous for locking students in the building overnight. It was rumored that once, he had even confined a student in the math wing for an entire Christmas break.

As the girls walked down the lonely hallway, they passed a poster for field day. "I can't believe there's an entire day devoted to three-legged races and potato-sack relays here," said Haley. "Public school is so weird."

"Not that I'll be participating," said Irene. "The seniors skip school that day, and there's a rumor they're convening at the Golden Dynasty around noon. I'm sure I'll be called in to help out my dad."

"So he lets you skip school to bus tables?"

"Yep. As if I don't have enough on my plate with

the yearbook cover and those posters for the Battle of the Bands . . ."

"Maybe I could help," Haley offered.

"We'll be okay," Irene said. "Shaun and Devon have already sworn they'll be there. And I'll kill them if they don't show."

"Well, at least let me extend your deadline for cover art by a few days," said Haley once they had reached the parking lot. She noticed her parents' hybrid SUV and realized Joan had been waiting patiently for hours. Haley wondered how long her mother would keep up the supermom routine. Probably until she took on her next big case. "Look, we've been really productive these past few days," Haley continued. "I've got some proofed pages that I can send to the printer early. That should buy us a little time with the cover."

"Thanks," Irene said reluctantly while unlocking her bike. Haley was astounded. Not only did Irene go to school, find time to develop her talents as an artist and work at her family's restaurant night after night, she also biked everywhere she went.

"Listen, why don't we throw your ride in the back of our car and my mom can drop you off at the Dynasty?" Haley suggested. Irene was about to protest when Haley added, "No way could I handle my cover artist being laid up by a bike accident right now."

Irene relented and let Haley take the handlebars.

And Haley noticed there seemed to be the slightest sense of relief on her friend's face.

● ● ●

All this time, everyone assumed Annie Armstrong was the biggest overachiever in Hillsdale High's sophomore class. Clearly, they all underestimated Irene.

But will Irene Chen's harried schedule of posters, and covers, and dirty plates in bus trays at the Dynasty inevitably lead to burnout? Is there anything Haley can do to lighten her friend's burden? And if she does decide to help Irene, will the *Talon* ever get published?

To help hostess and bus tables at the Dynasty on SENIOR SKIP DAY, turn to page 118. If you think the yearbook deadline is way more important than a bunch of rowdy seniors descending on a restaurant, skip to TURN IN PROOFS on page 93. Finally, isn't it high time Haley took a break herself? If you think so, send her to unwind at FIELD DAY on page 86.

There's a time for hard work and a time for play. Which time is it for Haley right now?

CONFRONT SEBASTIAN

**Boys are like eels.
The harder you try to hold on,
the easier it is for them
to slip away.**

"*Sebbie, mi favorito muchacho del mundo,***"** Mia Delgado said with great affection. Her luscious chestnut locks and bronzed skin glowed in the afternoon sun as the long-limbed Spanish beauty leaned in and kissed Sebastian on both cheeks.

Haley, who was shamelessly spying on the couple from the breezeway, seethed. She had already listened to Sebastian tell Mia in Spanish how much he'd missed her. When Sebastian took the gorgeous model in his arms in front of the whole school, it was just too much for Haley to take. She was, after all, his on-again-off-again American girlfriend, and she was not about to allow Sebastian to humiliate her like that.

Haley marched toward the lovers. "Sebbie!" she called out. "Oh, Sebbie! I've missed you too," she said, planting a kiss on his cheek. "Was it just last week that we were in Spain together? At your family's house? It feels like forever ago."

"You were in Spain, and you didn't tell me?" Mia asked, clearly offended.

"I . . . I . . . I thought you were traveling," Sebastian tried to explain.

"I would have come home."

"I'm Haley," Haley announced. "Sebastian's American girlfriend."

Mia frowned. She looked genuinely hurt.

"Haley, this is *mi . . . mi amiga* Mia," Sebastian said self-consciously.

"Oh, hi, '*mi amiqa Mia,*' " Haley said condescendingly. She turned back to Sebastian. "And how long has Mia been your *amiqa*?" she demanded, physically wedging herself between the two.

"What are you doing?" Sebastian said. He too, Haley noticed, seemed genuinely hurt, and taken aback by Haley's pushy and possessive behavior.

"We've known each other our whole lives," Mia chimed in. She stepped closer to Haley, trying to intimidate her with her height.

"How funny," Haley snapped back. "Sebastian

has never mentioned you. Ever. And we're really close."

Mia straightened her back. "Sebbie and I were neighbors as children. We were each other's first . . . everything," she concluded passionately. Sebastian reached out and took Mia's hand in solidarity.

Haley didn't know how to respond. She looked from Mia to Sebastian, frustrated by and jealous of the impenetrable bond between them. "You two deserve each other," she said finally. "Boy, am I glad Sebastian wasn't my first anything."

And with that, she stormed off. Sebastian didn't bother to say goodbye. He did, however, console Mia by inviting her to stay with him through the week. Which, Haley realized, probably would never have happened if she hadn't barged in on their parting moment and stirred up such an emotional reaction from her handsome Spaniard. Rumors soon began circulating that Mia and Sebastian had gotten back together. Then came news that Sebastian would be moving back to Spain a few weeks early, before the end of the school year.

When Haley realized she and Sebastian would never have a chance to reconcile, or even salvage a friendship, she felt like a fool. A very lonely fool.

● ● ●

Well, that was a slight disaster. Sebastian should've told Haley about his ex's visit for sure, even if nothing

romantic was going on between them. But Haley's handling of the situation didn't exactly help matters. Her clingy, presumptuous behavior drove Sebastian back into Mia's arms and ruined what was left of a budding relationship. It's an awful feeling when your own actions bring about your worst fears.

Time to go back to page 1 and start again.

GOOD HAIR DAY

If only good hair days were as predictable as dates on the calendar.

Haley bounded up the front steps out of the spring rainstorm and left her ballet flats, still damp from the grass, at the door. She stepped inside and was just starting to dry off when she spotted a stack of cardboard boxes overflowing with videotapes on the living room floor. Perry Miller emerged from the kitchen, his face beaming, a black marker in hand.

"Hey, Snoodles," he said cheerily, tousling Haley's wet hair before patting her on the head. "How was school today?"

"Um, good," she said, alarmed that her father was using one of her more ancient nicknames and showing affection in the way a parent might toward a toddler. "What's all this?" Haley inquired, though she didn't really need to ask. Whenever Perry finished one of his documentaries, he took on a major household project. And usually that household project had something to do with home movies.

"I found the most adorable footage of you today, Snoodles," Perry said, barely able to contain his excitement. "It's from your first trip to the zoo."

Uh-oh, Haley thought. *So much for getting Dad to extend my curfew by an hour.* With Perry sifting through old footage of her as a baby, it would be even harder to make him understand that she was growing up and it was time to let go.

"Why don't we watch something together?" he asked.

"Uh, sorry," said Haley, backing up slowly and racking her brain for an excuse. Who could say how many piano recitals were lurking in those boxes, ready to humiliate her if they slipped into the wrong hands? And she most definitely did not want to revisit her miniature self drooling in a high chair, or have to rewatch her infamous face-plant in her birthday cake at age four. "I've got to, uh . . . grab a snack. . . . Yeah, a snack . . . I'm about to pass out. School lunches, you know."

"Maybe tonight after supper, then?" Perry called out as she bolted into the kitchen.

Not on your life, Haley thought, discovering her mother in front of the stove wearing a red checkered apron and a starched white shirtdress, with perfectly coiffed hair. Joan was making her famous sheep's milk dumplings, something she usually only did about twice a year. On holidays. Or birthdays. This was a regular old Tuesday.

"Hi, dear," her mother said brightly, sounding a bit too Stepford for Haley's liking.

"Uh, homework. I have a ton" was all Haley managed to say as she grabbed some wheat crackers, sliced cheddar cheese and an apple, then headed up to her bedroom. "It'll probably take me all night."

"Don't work too hard, dear," Joan said. Haley didn't know whether she preferred the workaholic Joan or the robotic, devoted-to-my-family Joan. She just wished her normal mom would reappear.

Upstairs, Haley looked at the pile of assignments on her desk and decided against cracking any books right away. She then picked up her cell phone. *No calls, no texts, no love,* she thought. *Bo-ring.* She pondered her mother's radical new updo, then opened her knapsack and dumped out the spoils of a recent allowance splurge at the local pharmacy. There were a flat iron, a curling iron, headbands, a blow dryer and copious amounts of gels, styling mousses and hair sprays. The possibilities were split end—less.

Haley knew it was time for a change. The haircut she'd been forced to get a few months back, after Mitchell had stuck gum in her hair on a road trip, had finally grown out. But there was something heinous about the way the layers were now clumping around her face. She first thought about cutting it again, but instead decided styling was much more versatile and would allow her to change her look with her mood. What she was really hoping, though, was that a simple alteration in her appearance might finally catch the attention of a certain boy in her class. After all, nothing else had managed to do that.

Haley picked up her first tool and got to work.

● ● ●

To have Haley blow her hair out and straighten it like Sasha's, turn to BAND PRACTICE on page 129.

If you think Haley is secretly inspired by Annie Armstrong's new wavy mane, have her knock off Annie's sultry siren ways in TURN IN PROOFS on page 93.

If creating your own hairstyle is something you fear will go wrong no matter what you attempt, just throw on the preppy headband and meet Coco De Clerq for lunch at the local COUNTRY CLUB on page 105.

Lastly, if you think the hair spray and high-powered blow dryer would give Haley a little extra body, have her go out with attitude and a punky side ponytail on page 118 (SENIOR SKIP DAY).

The true athlete plays every point as if it's her last.

After school, Haley made her way over to the tennis courts, video camera in hand. Even though she wasn't exactly looking forward to filming Coco strutting around on the tennis court for the next few hours, financially speaking, it had been an offer she couldn't refuse. Coco was paying a hundred dollars a pop for documenting her tennis matches, so that her private tennis coach could analyze her game shot by shot.

Haley plopped down in the bleachers, trying to put some distance between herself and Coco's rough-looking entourage, Chopper and the Troll, two kids from the Floods who had recently become Ms. De Clerq's biggest fans. It wasn't that Haley didn't like them. She just didn't want their raucous cheering and eructations to drown out any score announcements or line calls on film. Haley was, after all, a professional, earning proper pay for her work.

"Co," Chopper called softly, standing up to lead the cheer.

"Co," the Troll answered quietly.

"Co," Chopper chanted louder, quickening the tempo.

"Co," the Troll called out.

After a few rounds of call-and-response, the boys broke into a locomotion rhythm.

"Co-co, Co-co, Co-co, Co-co," they chanted. Then Chopper threw his best train-whistle sound effect into the mix. "Woo-woo!"

Uh-oh, Haley thought. *This might just be the rowdiest tennis match Hillsdale has ever seen.* She steadied the tripod and angled the camera down toward the court, zooming in on Coco, who already had her game face on. Coco was barely acknowledging the crowd or the officials, much less her frightened-looking opponent, a reedy girl from Bergen North with stringy blond hair who seemed to keep muttering, *"That's Coco De Clerq."* The girl's babbling was understandable, Haley thought. Coco's gaze was beyond intimidating.

Whitney Klein was noisily making her way through the stands, heading in Haley's direction. As she got close, Whitney tripped on Haley's bag and spilled some of her gigantic fountain drink and pretzels.

"Whitney, watch the camera, please." Haley whispered the warning as the bubbly blonde took a seat next to her. Haley then pointed to the green On button on the camcorder, but Whitney didn't seem to notice or care.

"Ugh, look at that! Her arms look beefier already," Whitney exclaimed. "I told her all this tennis would be the end of sleeveless shirts."

"Whitney, shush," Haley said, getting back to work.

Down on the court, the game had just gotten under way. Coco broke her opponent's serve in the first game, and Haley realized it was basically over from there. The girl from Bergen North had already given up, maybe even before she stepped onto the court. But Coco never once let up, consistently demonstrating masterful focus, speed and agility, and of course that killer De Clerq backhand.

"You rock!" Chopper yelled as Coco drilled the ball down the line. The line judge called it in. On the next point, Coco smashed a crushing lob. "Marry me!" Chopper shouted, then melted to his knees.

After Coco had won her first set, defeating the former all-league player from Bergen North 6–1, she calmly dabbed her brow with a towel and switched sides of play. Haley followed, moving her camera equipment to the other side of the bleachers, with Whitney regrettably in tow.

"So when did you develop such an interest in tennis and/or Coco, anyway?" Whitney asked, trailing Haley and munching on a pretzel. "I mean, it's hard enough for me to sit through this stuff once. I can't imagine wanting to have it on tape."

"Coco's *paying* me to film her games," Haley explained, putting up a shade to block the glare from the late-afternoon sun. Chopper and the Troll grabbed seats next to them, then took off their shirts to reveal painted chests that each read c o.

"You mean to tell me you get *paid* to watch Coco play?" Whitney asked, clearly baffled. "No fair. Why am I not on her payroll?"

"Isn't it payment enough observing such grace and beauty on the court?" Chopper asked in all seriousness.

Not only is she paying me, she's taking me to lunch, Haley thought, though she figured it was probably best not to reveal to Whitney that Coco had invited Haley to a meal at the country club. It was, after all, only so she could deliver the video.

As Haley set up the tripod and prepared to record Coco's second set, she noticed Reese Highland, Cecily Watson and Sasha Lewis horsing around on the field after track practice. Sasha and Cecily were practicing the three-legged race, tripping their way across the grass as Reese ran alongside them and gave pointers. Haley felt a pang of jealousy, seeing the two girls laughing with Reese.

"Looks like someone's getting ready for field day," Whitney blurted out. "As far as I'm concerned, there couldn't be a lamer event. I'm definitely faking sick that day."

"Hey, shouldn't Sasha be at the Hedon's band practice?" the Troll observed, frowning. "What's she doing running *track*?"

Haley had noticed that everyone from the Floods was getting all riled up about the Hedon finally having a chance at defeating Rubber Dynamite in the Battle of the Bands. It was as if a win for the band would be a win for all of them, even though technically speaking, between Sasha and Toby, fifty percent of the band members were from the Hills. Haley wasn't so much worried about the Hedon's chances as she was curious to know how Sasha was managing to juggle all her extracurricular activities. *Then again,* Haley thought, *I should probably start worrying about my own life, not Sasha's or Whitney's or Coco's. I could be doing a lot more important things with my camera and my free time than filming someone's backhand for cash.*

● ● ●

Really, what is Haley doing here in the lonely hearts club? Sure, a hundred dollars for an afternoon of easy work is appealing. But she'll only go through high school once. Shouldn't she be out getting into trouble or having some fun?

What do you think? Is Haley getting jealous of all the track team camaraderie? Does she regret not going out for one of the few coed sports at Hillsdale High? If seeing that trio on the field makes Haley want to get in on the fun, flip to page 86, FIELD DAY.

Alternatively, if you think Haley should keep following Coco's rise to tennis stardom, go to the COUNTRY CLUB with her on page 105. Just be sure she doesn't end up using all her stardust on someone else.

**Front-row seats aren't always
the most desirable.**

Haley made her way to "the barn behind the school," the meeting spot Irene had arranged for them that afternoon. Most people would have just said "Meet me at the Snack Shack by the football field," but Irene didn't acknowledge anything about the game of football. Not even its concession stand.

Haley walked up to the bright red structure, which, during the Hawks' football season, did a steady business of sodas, hot dogs, chips and warm pretzels. The doors were now shuttered and locked, protecting the mascot's "nest" high up in the rafters. Haley couldn't help feeling a momentary pang of Hawks pride as she peered through the window and up at the ceiling beams, staring at the darkened thatch of straw. This only intensified when she turned around and caught sight of Reese Highland, Sasha Lewis and Cecily Watson running warm-up laps around the track.

Haley suddenly wondered if she'd made a huge mistake by not going out for the track team herself. But then Devon appeared from behind the Snack Shack with a mischievous look on his face. Haley got the feeling they were going to have a lot more fun this quarter than her friends who were gearing up to run timed miles.

"Hi there," Devon said, raising an eyebrow at her.

"What's gotten into you?" Haley asked, a bit be-wildered. Normally, it was a chore to get Devon to even look up from his thirty-five-millimeter camera, much less smile or say two words to her. His moody shyness had actually been the biggest and most con-sistent snag in their relationship to date. Haley would occasionally catch Devon at the right moment, and they would have a blast together. But then he would get called away to help out his family, watch his little sister or finish a new art project, and Haley would get dropped. She didn't know why she put up with it.

"Ask him about the call he just got from a New

York gallery," Irene suggested, popping up out of nowhere.

"Seriously?" Haley asked, turning to Devon. "You're getting a real show?"

"Well, not quite," Devon explained. "I'm being included in a roundup of student artists. But it's at a real space in Chelsea. With an opening and everything."

"That's great, Devon," Haley said, wrapping her arms around him for a hug. He let her for a moment, but then she felt him instinctively tense a little and pull away. *Here we go again, Mr. Tough Guy,* Haley thought.

"Thanks," he said briskly, staring off into the distance. He then added, in a somewhat annoyed tone, "So do you still need me to retake those photos of you or what?"

"Uh, I guess so. If it's not too much trouble." Haley turned to Irene and asked, "Why did you call us here, anyway?"

"To watch that," Irene said as Shaun burst forth from the locker rooms in a flash of gold and blue. He was dressed like a superhero, in a vintage disco-era tracksuit. Haley and the others indulged in a rare moment of watching Shaun *exercise*. He jiggled around the track, his slightly slimmer—but still very much there—spare tire undergoing a series of tectonic shifts every time one of his feet touched the pavement.

"Awesome," Irene whispered as Coach Tygert began scratching his head, trying to figure out whether Shaun was just a prankster or a legitimate candidate for the team.

Meanwhile, Shaun skipped wildly across the grass, stealing batons from relay runners and slaloming around hurdles. "Everything I do," Shaun belted out loudly, reaching out to slap the hands of Devon, then Haley and finally Irene as he passed, "I do it for you. Yeah, baby! Tsud ym tea! Tsud ym tea!"

"I'm swimming in it, Shauny," Irene said, smiling.

Watching them together, Haley wondered if she and Devon were the only ones left in Hillsdale who hadn't turned into complete fools for love this spring. Haley recalled an infomercial she had seen on late-night TV the previous week. It had been for a book and an accompanying "life system" that promised to change your destiny, if only you were ready to really concentrate on achieving your every goal and desire in life. Haley thought for a moment, then closed her eyes and willed Devon to notice her. She silently directed every atom in every molecule in every cell of her body to use their collective power to attract Devon McKnight to her, Haley Miller.

Instead, Devon just turned and asked Irene, "So, how are those band posters coming along?"

Haley felt deflated. And sleepy. Using all that willpower was exhausting.

"Eh," said Irene. "I'm not that thrilled with

them, but I just got a few sets back from the printer. Wanna see?"

Irene, Haley realized, had come quite a long way since she and Haley had met. Back then, Irene had been fiercely protective of her drawings, only showing them to the art teacher, Mr. Von, so she could get a passing grade in the class. Now she was about to paper the town with her work.

Of course, some things would never change, like Irene's job at the Golden Dynasty. She was already girding herself for field day, when the entire senior class was expected to turn up at her family's restaurant.

Haley looked down at the poster Irene was unrolling. THE BATTLE OF THE BANDS was written in pink letters along the bottom. Above that was Sasha Lewis's profile, silhouetted in white against a black background. Haley thought it was an instant classic but restrained herself from saying too much. Any sudden display of like or dislike and Irene might chicken out and not hang up a single one.

"I know just where we'll put this one," Devon said, grabbing the first print and a couple of poster nails from Irene's bag. He held it up on the wall of the Snack Shack and looked over at Irene, who grabbed the hammer, hesitated for a moment, then banged in the first nail.

Haley went to grab the next print but stopped when she noticed Reese Highland was watching her intently from the track. He smiled, waved and called out, "I hope I'll see you at field day this week."

Haley smiled and guiltily looked over at Devon, imagining what the rest of her spring might be like if she kept holding out for the brooding artist from the Floods . . . or if she started running with the athletic crowd and Reese.

● ● ●

Maybe Devon and Haley aren't cut out for each other after all. Is Devon getting tired of her? Or is he just still too shy to show his true feelings? And do you think Haley should keep trying to soften him up?

To send Haley to have her photo retaken by the master photographer and soon-to-be-showing-in-NYC Devon McKnight, turn to RESHOOTS WITH DEVON on page 113. If you think she'd better help out Irene at the Golden Dynasty on SENIOR SKIP DAY, turn to page 118. Finally, take Reese up on his invitation to FIELD DAY on page 86.

Some things are worth waiting for. But is one of those things Devon McKnight?

Having a normal school day
vs. a day of play?
No contest.

On the morning of field day, Ms. Lipsky wandered around homeroom wearing a navy blue skort, a sun visor and prescription sunglasses with amber lenses, making sure everyone was coated with the proper amount of sunscreen. "A pea-sized squirt for the face, and about a shot glass full for the body!" she reminded them, passing around plastic bottles filled with SPF 40 UVA/UVB protectant.

"Hear that, peeps?" Shaun called out, raising his eyebrows. "Body shots!"

Haley realized Ms. Lipsky wasn't taking official attendance, since Shaun was technically not in her homeroom. *Now I know why everyone considers coming to school for field day optional,* Haley thought, wondering what else she could have been doing with her day. But then Ms. Lipsky directed them out onto the field, Haley spotted Reese, Sasha, Johnny, Cecily and Drew, and she was content to be exactly where she was.

"The New Jersey Derby, up next!" Principal Crum announced over the bullhorn.

Principal Crum was wearing a kelly green polo shirt that looked just a *tad* too tight, short white shorts and a pair of pristine white sneakers, with his socks pulled up past his ankles.

"What's the New Jersey Derby?" Haley asked as she approached Sasha and Cecily's group.

"*This* is the New Jersey Derby," Drew said, getting down on all fours to demonstrate and letting Cecily mount his back as if she were riding a horse.

"Ah, dude, no way," Johnny said.

"Why not?" Sasha asked. "It'll be fun. Besides, I'm feeling competitive. I'm already going to whip these girls in the Best All Around category in class polls. Why not in the Jersey Derby, too?"

Sasha was referring to the fact that she, Haley and Cecily were all up for Best All Around in superlatives, which the school was currently voting on by grade. The girls had decided that joking about it was the only way to deal.

"What if I hurt my wrist?" Johnny asked. "Then where would we be for Battle of the Bands?" The upcoming Battle of the Bands was going to be the event of the season, according to, well, everyone. Sasha and Johnny's group, the Hedon, was going up against their longtime rival, Rubber Dynamite.

"You'll be fine," Sasha promised.

"Come on, bro, it's the *Derby*," Drew said. But Johnny was not obliging.

"Giddyup, cowgirl," Reese said to Haley, assuming the pony-ride position. She climbed on and they made their way over to the starting line, where Darla, the enormous senior who was on Haley's bus line to school, was trying to mount her latest skinny freshman boy toy. Darla kept smushing the boy into the mud.

"Is that even legal?" Haley asked.

"Do you think any teacher here is going to challenge Darla?" Reese asked. Finally, Darla switched positions and served as horse.

Once all the teams were in formation, Principal Crum held up his plastic cap gun. When the gun popped, the pairs took off, galloping toward the finish.

Haley held tight to Reese's shirt neck, amazed by how fast her "horse" was going. The grass was still damp from rain the previous night, and more and more jockeys were sliding off into the mud, including Darla's rider. Actually, it seemed as though Darla had purposely thrown him. Reese noticed that Drew and Cecily were gaining on them and picked up speed, galloping even faster. In the final stretch, with Cecily and Drew pulling up even, Reese stuck out his head and broke through the tape.

"By a nose!" the judge yelled, and pointed to Reese and Haley, waving a blue ribbon in the air along with the prize: gift certificates for free dinners at Hap's Diner.

"Thank you kindly," Reese said, standing up covered in mud to accept their spoils. Haley caught her breath just as Reese hoisted her up onto his shoulders for a victory lap. From that high vantage point, Haley located Sasha and Johnny, who were still standing at the starting line, arguing fiercely.

Haley next glanced over to the locker room doors and saw Hannah Moss sneaking into school. Reese turned, and Haley's view changed to the next station. Volunteer mothers were busy filling premade piecrusts with chocolate pudding and whipped-cream blobs.

"Awesome," Reese said, clearly eager to bank his next prize. "The pie-eating contest. I'm all *over* that one." He popped Haley off his shoulders, then held his stomach, signaling that it was time to chow down.

Shaun Willkommen was making his way over to the pie-eating station too. *Reese doesn't stand a chance if Shaun is competing,* Haley thought. Shaun had, after all, recently won the biggest Hap's challenge in Hillsdale's history. But then, much to Haley's surprise, Shaun passed right by the sign-up table and took a front-row seat in the audience. *Wow, he must really be serious about that diet he's on,* Haley realized.

Reese took yet another first prize after downing twenty-two plates of chocolate and cream. Haley thought he might need a break after that competition, but no, Reese was anxious to make it to the dunking booth station, where a crowd had already gathered around in anticipation of the first toss of the baseball and the chance to watch a teacher get dunked.

"The goal is to hit the red bull's-eye," Ms. Frick announced. "Who will be the first to dunk Principal Crum in the *agua fría*?"

Reese handed her one of his tickets and grabbed his bin of three rubber balls. He concentrated hard, took aim and launched the first ball. It brushed against the target but didn't hit the bull's-eye. Principal Crum wobbled a little in his seat. "Nice one, Highland," Principal Crum said cockily.

Reese picked up the second ball. "If I make this one, will you come over to study tonight?" he asked Haley.

"I'll take my chances," Haley said. This ball connected with the bull's-eye, and the principal fell into the chilly water.

"Highland, remember, I sign your report cards,"

he said, climbing back into the hot seat just in time for Reese to dunk him again. The crowd roared as Principal Crum, already wet and dripping, fell back into the tank.

In all the commotion, Haley collided with a fast-moving Hannah Moss, who was scurrying away from the school building. Hannah dropped the stack of papers she was carrying into the mud, so Haley bent down and helped her collect them. As Haley handed over the muddied sheets, she saw that they were forms. Class polls, actually.

"Thanks," Hannah said, looking around furtively, then continued on her way.

I wonder what she's up to, Haley thought as she watched Hannah slip into the parking lot, somehow sure that those forms were not supposed to be in Hannah's possession.

● ● ●

Does it seem so unlikely that Haley would have a shot at being chosen Best All Around in the sophomore class? She is, after all, pretty darn great. Plus, she's dating the cutest, most popular boy in her class. But if she wins, how will that affect her friendships with Sasha and Cecily? And what if the honor isn't legit?

To find out more about what's going on with the class polls, tune in to Dave Metzger's "Inside Hillsdale," where he'll be PODCASTING THE POLLS (page 133) and revealing all the latest updates.

Two girls who until recently would have had most of the good categories locked up were missing from field day entirely. Where were Whitney Klein and Coco De Clerq? And what are they up to these days? To find out, skip to HOLEY HOBBY on page 97.

Meanwhile, that sounded like an awfully tempting invite from Reese Highland. Do you think Haley should go STUDY WITH REESE on page 124? What will happen when the two are finally alone in his room together?

Finally, make sure everything is okay between Sasha and Johnny by visiting their BAND PRACTICE on page 129. Some couples make beautiful music together. Others just make a lot of noise.

TURN IN PROOFS

**Sometimes the hardest part
of finishing a project
is simply letting it go.**

The yearbook proofs were almost ready for the printer. All that was left to do were the class superlatives. Even so, it was hard for Haley to think about actually turning the project in. *What if there are a hundred mistakes we didn't catch?* Haley thought. *What if we left out a page? What if everyone hates the theme?*

On the day the committee was supposed to do a final walk-through with the staff yearbook advisors, Haley procrastinated by experimenting with a new hairstyle before school. She played around with a curling iron until her fine auburn locks had been transformed into a mane of long, loose curls. It wasn't going to keep the yearbook walk-through from happening, but at least if she did fail, she would look pretty trying.

On her way to Ms. Lipsky's classroom, Haley felt her phone vibrate. Glad for the delay, she stopped and saw she had two messages. One was from Irene Chen, apologizing for having to skip the last committee meeting; she needed to help Shaun practice for his first big track meet—which she was inviting Haley to, Haley was surprised to see. The other text was from Reese Highland, asking her if she wanted to study together for the upcoming history final. Both invitations sounded appealing.

"Greetings, fellow Talonites," Haley said to the committee once everyone had arrived. "Today will be our final call to order." The room erupted with applause. "Okay, okay, I can see the troops are getting restless. Let's finish up with these polls and put this baby to bed."

Haley noticed Annié Armstrong and Dave Metzger sitting near the back of the room, of course, wrapped up in each other like a human pretzel. Naturally, they were counting the votes for Best Couple in each grade. The girl with the braids, whom Haley had increasingly come to rely on since she took such good direction, was working on Most Popular, from her class through seniors. And Hannah Moss had commandeered the Best All Around category across the board, of particular importance since Haley was one of the sophomore nominees.

After all the ballots had been distributed, a hush fell over the room, and everyone began to count. Haley sat down and began to add up her votes for Most Likely to Succeed, but it was difficult to concentrate. About ten minutes into the silence, she heard the sound of rustling papers, looked up and saw that the disturbance was coming from Hannah Moss. *What is she doing?* thought Haley. *Is she . . . stuffing ballots into her book bag? Nah, impossible.*

Besides, it was time to collect the results. Arrangements had been made to podcast the poll results live on "Inside Hillsdale" that afternoon, though given Dave's current level of distraction, Haley wondered if he'd be able to keep up with his podcast at all. *Thank goodness they'll soon be out of my hair,* Haley thought, watching the duo make out. What a relief it would be to no longer have to deal with the yearbook committee, and all the annoying headaches that came with chairing it.

● ● ●

Well, Haley seems to have pulled off the impossible. The yearbook proof is ready to go to the printers, no thanks to Annie Armstrong.

If you are too excited for words and just can't wait

another second to hear who's won this year's polls—and see if Haley was chosen as Best All Around!—find out the results live in PODCASTING THE POLLS on page 133. Alternatively, if you think Haley's job here is done, send her to STUDY WITH REESE on page 124.

Now that Haley no longer has to keep a Hawk Eye on her yearbook committee minions, however will she fill her days? That, my dear, is up to you.

HOLEY HOBBY

**Finding a needle in a haystack
is nothing compared to
stitching up a couture gown.**

Haley hadn't seen much of Whitney Klein around
school lately. And now that Coco De Clerq was focus-
ing on the upcoming regional tennis tournament, ignoring all her old friends, Haley hadn't had much
cause to see Whitney *outside* of school either, as there
were no longer any Coquette expeditions to tag along
on. So one afternoon, Haley decided to head over to
the Floods and check up on Hillsdale High's resident
clotheshorse.

"Haley!" Linda Klein, Whitney's mother, greeted

her enthusiastically from the landing of their sketchy apartment building.

Wow, she's chipper, Haley thought, smiling and waving back. *I wouldn't be that psyched about living in this dump.*

"Whitney's inside, dear. How are you? And how are your parents?"

Huh, Haley thought, taking note of Mrs. Klein's new attitude and newly svelte body. *I wonder if the divorce finally came through?*

Sure enough, Mrs. Klein stepped aside and Haley saw that she was standing next to a stack of cardboard boxes and a big roll of bubble wrap.

"I'm okay," Haley replied. "More importantly, how are you?"

"Couldn't be better, Haley," Linda said, loading a pair of vases into a box. "I'm finally moving on with my life!"

And what a life it was. The whole saga was a bit *too* soap opera–ish, as far as Haley was concerned. Linda Klein was divorcing Jerry Klein, New Jersey's breath-spray king, because he had cheated on her with a woman named Trish, a much-younger waitress from the local country club. While in the throes of a depression over the split, and over having to move to the Floods because Jerry had frozen all her assets, Linda had started attending AA meetings, though she wasn't really an alcoholic. "It's the only form of therapy she can afford," Whitney had explained to Haley.

While in the group, Linda had reconnected with Mr. Lewis, Sasha Lewis's father, who himself was recovering from a severe gambling and alcohol addiction. The two began dating, but only after Linda fessed up about her non–drinking problem. It didn't take long for them to decide to move in together as soon as Linda's divorce was settled, though Mr. Lewis's sponsor had discouraged the idea. Somewhere in the middle of all that, Whitney had developed a shoplifting habit, and Sasha's mother had returned to Hillsdale from Paris.

Haley could barely keep it all straight.

In the Kleins' tiny apartment, Haley saw that the kitchen cupboards had been emptied. In the living room were linens sorted by color and size, and all the pictures had been taken down from the walls. Haley guessed the Kleins would be out within the week. She knocked on Whitney's bedroom door.

"Un segundo," Whitney called out.

When she finally opened up, Whitney had a needle and thread in her hand, and she was standing next to a mannequin wearing a partially finished, and actually quite cute, green and white circle skirt.

"What's going on in here?" Haley asked playfully, but also with a little awe. It was surprising enough that Whitney and her mom were finally moving out of their shoe-box apartment and out of the Floods, but Haley found it far more shocking that (a) Whitney owned a needle and thread and (b) she actually knew how to use them.

"I'm just . . . fooling around," Whitney explained with a shrug. She pulled a pin from the satin pincushion on her desk, then stuck it into the mannequin's skirt, tightening it at the waist.

Haley glanced at the half-packed boxes and saw a sketch pad full of patterns, swatches of fabric and pages torn from glossy fashion magazines. "This doesn't look like fooling around to me."

"Yeah, I guess I am pretty serious."

Something sleek and shiny on the side table next to Whitney's bed caught Haley's eye. It was a brand-new sewing machine. "Where'd you get *that*?" Haley asked somewhat skeptically. Whitney had, after all, recently developed a fondness for taking things that didn't belong to her.

"My mom bought it for me," Whitney explained. "When she got the settlement check."

Haley examined the craftsmanship on the skirt. Instead of simply using a patterned fabric, Whitney had cut holes or large polka dots out of the white fabric and backed them with green scraps, leaving the exposed seams slightly unfinished. The mixture of machine work and meticulous hand stitching was impressive. "This is incredible, Whitney," Haley marveled.

"That's nothing," Whitney said, pulling another garment from the closet. "The beadwork alone on this gown took me over twenty hours. They're vermincello beads."

"You mean vermicelli." Haley couldn't believe her eyes. Whitney had designed and sewn a pale blue evening gown shimmering with crystals as clear as the Caribbean. It was a little on the pageanty side, sure. But then, so were most of Whitney's tastes.

"I'm convinced this sewing machine is the only good thing that will come out of us moving in with Mr. Lewis," Whitney confessed. "I mean, besides getting out of this ghetto Floods apartment."

"Aren't they moving a bit fast?" Haley said, thinking out loud. It was pretty contagious around Whitney.

"What, because of his alcohol and gambling addictions, and because my mom is still recovering from . . . Trish?"

Haley nodded.

"Well, they say they're in love," Whitney replied, clearly resigned to her fate. "I tried talking some sense into her. Then I tried talking some sense into him. But as you can see, that didn't quite work. I just hope it lasts long enough for my mom to buy her own place."

"Well, this ought to cheer you up," Haley said, plopping down on Whitney's bed and handing her a copy of the school paper, opened to its "Hawk Talk" gossip section. "It looks like you're the favorite to win Best Dressed in the class polls this year."

"Really?" Whitney asked, snatching up the broadsheet. "Oooooh!" Whitney squealed. "I smell a comeback!" Suddenly, Whitney's face darkened. "Hey, it says here you're up for Best All Around."

Haley blushed. "I'm sure they got that totally wrong. There are also rumors going around saying that nominations were rigged, Crum is investigating, and Annie Armstrong has been slacking off so much there might not even *be* a yearbook. Can you *believe*?"

"Does Coco know she's competing against you?"

"Yeah, um, about that . . . ," Haley said, hesitating. "Coco isn't up for anything this year."

"Whoa." Whitney sat down on her bed.

"I know," Haley replied. "Do you think we should tell her?"

"No way," Whitney said solemnly. "We're lucky she's got tennis to focus on right now. Otherwise, she would be taking this out on us. Just mark my words, though—one of these days Coco's going to snap out of it, and then you and I are going to have the old Coco De Clerq to deal with."

Haley shuddered at the thought.

Out the window and down on the street, Haley watched as a girl with dark hair pedaled furiously by on her bike. "Isn't that . . . Irene Chen?" Haley asked.

"Ugh, probably," Whitney said, exasperated. "She, like, totally thinks I'm one of them now. Just because we've been staying in this hovel *temporarily*. I mean, hello? I'm still Whitney Klein. Do you know last week she even tried to get me to *work* at her dad's restaurant with her? Can you imagine? Just because I like to eat there a lot—they do have really good dim sum—and I was *temporarily* without an allowance. But that doesn't mean I would have been willing to, like, bus tables on the day the whole senior class crashed the place. I mean, does she really think I'd even consider . . ."

Whitney's voice trailed off in Haley's mind. *Gosh, Irene must have been really desperate if she asked Whitney for help,* Haley thought. *Though I guess I would have been too if several hundred rowdy seniors had crashed my family's restaurant while the rest of the school was busy with field day. Maybe she's the one I should be checking on instead of Whitney. Everything seems okay here.*

● ● ●

That was certainly an ominous statement about Coco De Clerq. Do you think her tennis game is just a temporary distraction? Is the old Coco bound to return?

If you're brave enough to find out, turn to *V IS FOR VANQUISHED* on page 139. If you'd rather check in on the overworked and underappreciated Irene, visit THE CHEN HOUSEHOLD on page 144. Finally, if you're dying to find out the results of the class polls, whether or not they were rigged, turn to PODCASTING THE POLLS on page 133.

Will Haley be named Best All Around? Will the yearbook even be published? And will everyone at Hillsdale High soon be wearing Whitney Klein's designs? Read on to find out.

There's absolutely nothing "country" about a country club.

Haley decided to skip field day and meet Coco at the Bergen County Country Club for lunch. The invitation had only been extended so that Haley could deliver videos of Coco's most recent match to the tennis instructor at the club. But the allure of finding out what life was like on the other side of BCCC's fifteen-foot-high green hedges was too tempting for Haley to pass up.

She deliberated about her hair and ended up wearing a new headband, because it seemed like preppy was the safest way to go. Haley paired that with a grosgrain-belted denim skirt that went to the knee and one of Mitchell's baby blue button-downs with the sleeves rolled up to her elbows. It was way Waspy but cute. Once she made it past the ridiculously strict security gates—the guards practically asked Haley to provide fingerprints and submit to an eye scan—she was led down a long wood-paneled hall to the clubhouse, where Coco was in deep discussion with a handsome guy in a pale yellow polo.

Hello! Haley thought. *If that's Coco's instructor, no wonder she's so into tennis.*

"Haley, this is Brad," Coco said, making the introduction in a businesslike fashion. "We have a table on the veranda." Coco walked briskly in front of them as Brad and Haley exchanged polite smiles and tried to keep up.

"Nice to meet you," said Haley, shaking Brad's hand.

"Likewise," said Brad, pulling out a chair for her.

"We'll have three Cobb salads, a fresh fruit plate and a large bottle of still water, ice cold," Coco instructed one of the servers as they sat down in the yellow-awning-covered space. Haley was expecting to at least be offered a menu, but Coco explained, "We don't have much time. Brad and I have a court at two."

"Why don't we have a look at this video?" Brad suggested.

Haley opened her bag and took out her digital camcorder and laptop computer. By the time the salads arrived, she had linked the two with a firewire and then put up a montage of Coco's strokes. Brad and Coco watched intently, occasionally glancing at each other and nodding in agreement, without even having to speak.

"It's all here, just like you asked," Haley said, showing them a glimpse of the full game in real time, along with the spliced-together footage Coco had requested. Haley handed Coco and Brad each their own copy of the DVD.

"This looks great, Miller," Brad said. "I should hire you to film all my clients."

"Sure," said Haley, "as long as you keep paying me this well."

Brad was already getting up from the table to attend to a demanding-looking middle-aged woman who was in her tennis whites and standing by the bar looking peeved. "Haley, nice meeting you," he said, excusing himself. "Tigre, we'll talk on the court, okay?"

Tigre? Haley thought. *Just how private do Brad's lessons get?* The older woman at the bar was chiding him and glaring jealously at Coco and Haley.

"This salad is terrible," Coco announced. "I hate the new chef. Let's get club sandwiches at the Nineteenth Hole."

"Sure," Haley agreed, not quite sure what the

Nineteenth Hole was but game to find out. She followed Coco past the golf course and into the club's *second* outdoor café, where they grabbed a table under a huge white and yellow striped umbrella.

"I can't stand cougars," said Coco, by way of explanation for their sudden change of venue. "Just because these women pay Brad for lessons, they think they somehow own him."

Cougars? Haley thought. She was beginning to think country club–speak was its own dialect.

"Cougars are almost as bad as vultures. You know, those senior guys who prey on freshmen and sophomores because they assume we're all easy."

"You mean like Richie Huber?"

"Precisely. Just watch, Haley. I bet we both get asked to the prom."

A waitress appeared, and Coco once again rattled off an order without bothering to ask Haley what she might like. "Two clubhouse sandwiches, two Arnold Palmers with no ice, extra lemon." Within moments, two iced teas mixed with lemonade were set down on the table.

Looking around the club grounds, Haley felt as if she were at some kind of five-star resort. It certainly didn't seem like New Jersey, much less Hillsdale. The grass was perfectly manicured. The greens rolled in all directions. *Of course, I can only imagine how much pesticide they're dumping around here to keep it so pristine,* Haley thought, clearly her mother's daughter.

They had a prime view of the main clubhouse, where Haley spotted Spencer Eton, who also seemed to be skipping out on field day. Spencer was wearing a tie and walking with his mother and two finely suited men. Next to them was . . . Coco's sister, Ali De Clerq.

Coco noticeably bristled when she spotted the group.

"So you and Spencer haven't been hanging out much lately," Haley observed.

"He's got his mother's campaign," Coco said flatly, her eyes still on everything but her sister and the seemingly reformed cad. "I'm on the court three hours a day. I barely see my parents."

"It does seem like it would be hard, giving up so much for a sport. Family, your friends. When was the last time you saw Whitney?" Haley asked. She was surprised, actually, not to find Coco's lifelong sidekick hovering around them. Coco glanced around, as if she too expected Whitney to be standing nearby.

"She charged a few too many Arnold Palmers on her father's past-due account, and now they won't let her in here," said Coco, sipping her drink. "And Mrs. Klein's membership was revoked ages ago."

"Poor Whitney," Haley said, knowing that access to the country club was as important as bread or water to their friend. It was yet another blow for the girl who had been caught shoplifting a few weeks back. Her dad was also having a midlife crisis in the form of an affair with a barely-out-of-adolescence waitress, and rumor had it that Mrs. Klein was now thinking of moving in with Sasha Lewis's recovering-alcoholic father. "I wonder if she got stuck at field day," Haley suggested. "Can you imagine Whitney in a three-legged race?"

"Wait, she did text me this morning. Something about getting a present from her mom, to celebrate the divorce coming through and moving out of the Floods. I think it was a . . . sewing machine. Sad, really."

"I don't know," Haley said. "A sewing machine might be good for Whitney. She *does* love clothes. And she can't keep taking them when they don't belong to her."

The waitress came out with their club sandwiches. Before she could set them down, Spencer appeared and lifted a sandwich wedge off Coco's plate.

"Well, if it isn't the ladies who lunch," Spencer said mockingly. He looked handsome in his shirt and tie, Haley thought, hating herself for noticing.

"Don't you have palms to squeeze or babies to kiss?" Coco asked icily.

"Anything for the campaign," Spencer said with faux seriousness. "By the way, congrats, Haley."

Coco tensed. "Okay, I'll bite. What are we congratulating her for?"

"Haven't you heard?" said Spencer, feigning innocence. "She's up for Best All Around in the class polls. Word is, she's got the title all locked up. I mean, since you're not nominated this year."

The color drained from Coco's face. Haley knew Coco wasn't up for a single category, and she also knew that being passed over probably didn't sit too well with the former teen queen.

"Did I say something to offend?" Spencer asked. "Well, back to the salt mines. You would not believe how boring it is to sit through a two-hour meal while some cretin who owns a car dealership complains about the state's emissions laws."

I'm going to pretend I didn't hear that, Haley thought, imagining her mother's reaction. She took a gulp of her drink and didn't say another word.

● ● ●

There's a finer side to life in Hillsdale, which the Miller family is blissfully unaware of. Now that Haley has gotten a taste of country club perks, will she be able to go back to life without Arnold Palmers, Cobb salads and the Nineteenth Hole?

If you think Haley's at home with the lunching set, go film Coco at her next match in *V IS FOR VANQUISHED* on page 139. If you think the club atmosphere is a little too stuffy for Haley and are more interested in finding out if she was named Best All

Around in the sophomore class, turn to PODCASTING THE POLLS on page 133.

It's too bad Spencer and Coco can't seem to get together as a couple. Two selfish, manipulative wrongs might just make a right. Will Haley ever find her perfect other half? And is he, like Spencer, just under her nose?

RESHOOTS WITH DEVON

Everyone deserves
at least one, maybe even two,
second chances.

Haley headed over to the Spanish classroom and the unofficial eleventh-hour reshoots for the *Talon's* yearbook photos. Even though a fellow student was taking the photos—the supercute Devon McKnight— Haley wasn't at all worried about how the shots would turn out. Anything, absolutely anything, would be better than her original portrait, so what did she have to lose?

Devon had already set up the professional camera equipment he'd rented. There was a flash box, a big camera on a tripod, booms, clamps and focus lights, which he was busy angling into position as Haley entered the room.

"Impressive," she said, nodding.

"Great, you're early. Could you sit down over on that stool for me?" Devon instructed in a businesslike fashion. He picked up a large metallic dish that looked as if it was made of tinfoil and began to move it around.

"What's the flying saucer for?" Haley teased, sitting down in front of the backdrop of a large roll of soft blue paper.

"To lighten up your face. Not that you need much, Ms. Best All Around."

Haley blushed. "It's only a nomination," she said, referring to the sophomore-class superlatives, which were being voted on that week. "The final ballots haven't even been counted yet."

"From what I hear, you've got it all locked up."

Haley suddenly felt a familiar nervousness creep over her as she looked into the lens. "That's a really big camera."

"Pro rental's on the school's dime. I'm in heaven," Devon added, stepping behind the machine. "Okay, I'm ready to fire off a few tests."

"What do I do?" Haley asked.

"Just . . . be yourself," said Devon.

Great, Haley thought. *That's what got me into trouble the last time.*

Haley had a long history of seizing up in front of the camera, particularly during yearbook photos. Even though her dad was a filmmaker, and thus had made photo and video records of every stage of Haley's life, she had never really reached a point where she was comfortable being captured on film. If anything, she'd grown *less* comfortable over the years, just as she'd grown more and more adept at shooting other people.

Haley self-consciously tucked a strand of hair behind her ear. "That's nice," said Devon, looking through the lens. Haley pursed her lips, and the color rose in her cheeks.

Devon started clicking off shots. The bounce dish he'd propped up against a desk chair doused her with a flash of light, and she cringed a little.

"You know what?" Devon said, standing up for a moment. "I'm going to lose the flash and just shoot you with natural light."

"Won't that mess up the continuity in the yearbook?"

"Not if we do this right," he said, glancing at a light meter and readjusting the foil disc. Devon returned to the camera and began to shoot again. "That's great," he said as Haley dropped her shoulders and relaxed her posture. He worked quickly and encouraged her. She tossed her hair back playfully, put her chin down and gazed right into the camera. Devon snapped away.

"Well, I think we got it," he finally said as he finished his roll.

"That's it?" asked Haley. She felt a twinge of disappointment that their moment together was over. That was new—she was usually itching to flee before, during and after a photo session.

"*Something* in here will work, trust me," Devon said, holding up the film, then resetting all the equipment for his next subject. "Not that it even matters. From what I hear, Annie Armstrong is so slacking off on her yearbook duties, there might not even be a *Talon*."

"At least my parents will have something nice to hang on the wall," Haley said, backing out of the room. She turned around to go, then spun back around on her heel. "Are you by chance free for dinner tomorrow?" she asked impulsively.

Devon looked up and smiled. "Nope," he said, shutting her down. Haley felt crushed. "I'm due at Irene's house. Her grandmother's cooking a traditional meal for us. But you're welcome to come, as my date."

Haley went crimson. She was completely tongue-tied. Although she knew exactly how to answer.

● ● ●

Well, that wasn't so bad, now, was it? Finally, Haley takes a good yearbook photo. She almost seemed to be enjoying that session toward the end. Clearly, the right photographer makes all the difference.

But what if Devon was speaking the truth about the yearbook? If Haley is named Best All Around, will she even get to enjoy the accolades if the *Talon* doesn't make it to press on time? And will her perfect picture be seen by anyone except her mom and dad?

If you think Haley should take Devon up on his offer of a dinner date, turn to THE CHEN HOUSEHOLD on page 144. If Haley is more interested in finding out who was named Best All Around in her class, turn to POD-CASTING THE POLLS on page 133.

Will Haley opt for a private romantic moment or aim for public glory? And which form of success do you think would make her happier?

SENIOR SKIP DAY

Good things come
to those who waitress.

On the morning of what was supposed to be the schoolwide field day, Irene Chen forwarded Haley an e-mail entitled SENIOR SKIP DAY: THE GOLDEN DYNASTY. The recipient list included the entire senior class, and it looked as though they all planned to smuggle flasks of alcohol and even fireworks into Irene's family's restaurant.

Haley knew Irene rarely asked anyone for help, even if she desperately needed it. So, deciding it was her duty to skip field day too and bail out Irene,

Haley showed up at the Golden Dynasty that morning ready to bus tables, pour water, clean up the buffet, serve food or do whatever it took to keep her friend from getting completely slammed and have disaster befall the family business.

Irene wasn't in her usual spot behind the cash register. Haley heard pots and pans clanking in the kitchen and decided to investigate. She found Mr. Chen in the middle of the kitchen, teaching an aproned Devon McKnight how to make egg rolls. Devon smiled and held up his spatula when Haley poked her head in.

"Thank God," said Irene, sighing with relief. "You have no idea how glad I am to see you," she added, emerging from the linen closet with a stack of tablecloths. "We just heard half of the junior class is cutting too, and that stomach flu that's been going around has two-thirds of my dad's staff at home in bed."

At an empty table by the bar, Irene gave Haley a stack of clean napkins. "Don't worry about folding them like swans. Just get them on the tables," she said.

Just then, there was a jingle at the door.

"Here we go," Irene said cautiously. "Haley, all the pitchers are on that station behind you. You saw where the ice machine is in the kitchen?"

"I'm on it," said Haley.

Shaun Willkommen appeared at the front of the restaurant.

"Where have you been?" Irene asked, visibly relieved.

"What a cuddly welcome kind, gets the Shaun," he said, speaking in Yoda.

Shaun's gold track pants had huge grass stains streaked across the knees, and his white T-shirt looked damp. Clearly, he'd run all the way from early track practice. Irene walked Shaun over to the restrooms, where he could wash up before any customers arrived.

Just after the clock struck noon, the entire restaurant filled up with rowdy members of the junior and senior classes. Irene smartly made them all prepay—with a sizeable tip—as they came in, since she figured they would soon be too drunk and out of hand to divide up any bills.

"Haley? What are you doing here?" Ali De Clerq scoffed as Haley poured ice water into her glass at a large round table of locally famous senior girls and guys. "Shouldn't you be, like, following my little sister around and filming her tennis lessons or something?"

"Uh, you're confusing me with Whitney Klein," said Haley, moving to the next table of raucous students and topping off their water glasses. Not that anyone would actually drink it. Still, Irene had stressed how important it was to give them the option during the boozefest. The last thing they needed was a vomithon line in the bathroom.

When she got to his table, Richie Huber grabbed Haley by the arm and said, "Hey, you're cute. Maybe I should ask you to prom." She ignored him and moved on.

As the lunch rush hit its peak, everyone was juggling at high speeds, trying to keep the food coming out of the kitchen as quickly as possible, busing the tables so the place didn't get completely trashed. Devon and Mr. Chen had a two-man assembly line going and were whipping out orders of sesame chicken and moo shu pork. Meanwhile, Irene, Haley and Shaun kept the buffet stocked and ran plates of hot food out to the tables, in between delivering soft drinks and carrying away dirty dishes. Surprisingly, things were running pretty smoothly, though Haley realized that with just one fewer pair of hands, it would have been disastrous.

Haley spotted Whitney Klein by the cash register, waiting impatiently. Haley glanced over at Irene, who was carrying a heavy banquet tray stacked eight plates high with dirty dishes. Shaun was lugging what looked to be an equally heavy chafing dish of seafood medley to the buffet. *Guess I'm on take-out duty,* Haley decided.

"Welcome to the Golden Dynasty," Haley said, forcing a smile for Whitney. "Can I help you?"

"Haley?" Whitney said, confused to see her friend working at the restaurant. "I didn't know you worked here. I mean, I didn't know you worked."

"It's a *temporary* arrangement," Haley replied. "I take it you didn't go to field day either?"

"You know how I feel about sweating in public." Haley saw a few stray strands of pink thread stuck to Whitney's crisp white shirt—unusual, since Whitney was always immaculately dressed. So much so that she was up for Best Dressed in the class polls, while Haley was miraculously a candidate for Best All Around. "Speaking of sweating in public," Whitney added, "are you coming to watch Coco in the regionals?"

"I don't know," said Haley, handing Whitney her to-go bag. "I'll have to see about that."

"Well, there's a lot we have to catch up on," Whitney said mysteriously before leaving the restaurant with a wave.

Just then, a girl over at one of the junior tables let out a bloodcurdling scream. A meathead senior Haley recognized from the football team had just chucked an egg roll clear across the room and accidentally hit the girl smack in the head. Before there was retaliation from any of the junior guys, Haley ran over to quell the conflict. She was ready to do whatever it took to make sure no food fights broke out on her watch.

● ● ●

Devon now knows how to make egg rolls? How cool. Haley can balance six water pitchers on a tray? If their art careers don't work out, this little crew could open their own restaurant. Just how *temporary* do you think this arrangement is? Would Haley ever get a real job at the Golden Dynasty to make some extra cash? Or was she just helping Irene out this once?

If you want to stick with Irene, Shaun and Devon, have a celebratory dinner at THE CHEN HOUSEHOLD on page 144. If you think hanging out with Whitney and watching Coco kick butt on the tennis court sounds more appealing, flip to *V IS FOR VANQUISHED* on page 139.

The *I Ching* may be able to give you hints about what's in store, but Haley's destiny is really up to you. So what does her future hold?

STUDY WITH REESE

Boyfriends and books can be a tricky combination.

"Mom, we're going upstairs to study," Reese shouted as he dragged Haley through the front door and up to his bedroom. "Big history test next week. Huge."

"Hello, Mrs. Highland," Haley called out, not wanting to be impolite. "My mother said to say hi."

Barbara Highland, Reese's petite brunette mother, came out of the kitchen and said, "Hi, Haley. Nice to see you. And good luck, you two."

Haley had never actually been in Reese's bedroom

before, though she certainly knew the layout. Her bedroom window faced his, and it was hard not to occasionally catch a glimpse of a yawning Reese pulling up the shade in the morning or drawing it back down at night. Haley wondered if Reese ever stole similar glances at her in her nightgown.

"You thirsty?" Reese asked, grabbing two sodas from his minifridge and tossing one to Haley.

"Sure," she said, cracking hers open and taking a sip.

Reese plopped down on the bed. His history notebooks and textbook were on the nightstand, but he didn't seem too interested in opening them right away. Haley tentatively took a seat on the edge of the bed, not too far from his right knee.

"So, you ready for this big track meet on Saturday?" Haley asked.

"Totally," Reese said, looking pumped. "Especially since I can't wait to see the girls' relay team kick some serious butt." He winked and let his knee fall so that it gave Haley a gentle nudge in the ribs, tickling her side. She relaxed against him on the bed. "You like the pad?" Reese asked, gesturing around the room.

"Actually . . ." Haley paused, considering whether to reveal the view from her bedroom. "I've seen it before."

"Oh really?" Reese said, smiling. He shifted on

the bed so that they were facing each other. "And when was that?"

"Haven't you noticed? Our bedroom windows face each other," Haley whispered playfully.

"Oh, I've noticed," said Reese, nodding with his eyebrows raised.

"Hey," said Haley, giving his arm a soft punch. "What's that supposed to mean?"

"It means I definitely hope our parents don't decide to move." And with that, Reese leaned over and kissed Haley, pressing his lips to her mouth, her nose, her ears. "Come here, Ms. Best All Around." It was true, and somehow miraculous: Haley had indeed won the title for the sophomore class, beating out both Sasha and Cecily. Though the results would likely never be printed. It was looking more and more as if there wouldn't be a *Talon* this year, thanks to the non-efforts of type-A-turned-slacker Annie Armstrong.

Haley pulled back a little. "What about your mom?" she asked Reese, looking at the door.

"Don't worry," Reese said, kissing her again. "I get a carb-loaded meal in preparation for every track meet. She'll be in the kitchen for *hours*." Reese's arms wrapped around Haley's waist, and he kissed her again as she melted into his embrace.

Making out with Reese didn't make Haley the least bit anxious, because he never pushed her to go too far. Reese thought high school was far too early for a serious physical relationship. Which meant Haley never had to face that decision.

"How is Sasha going to make it through the meet *and* the Battle of the Bands?" Haley asked, her head resting on Reese's chest.

"If anyone can pull it off, it's Sasha," Reese said. He leaned in again for another kiss, then did something unusual. He placed his hand on Haley's stomach and slowly undid a few of the buttons on her shirt.

"Um, maybe we should look over our history notes," Haley said, stiffening in his arms. This was foreign territory to her, and she wasn't sure if she was ready to make the trip.

"Sure," Reese said softly, kissing her forehead before sitting up and grabbing the stack of books from the nightstand. "Where should we begin?"

A cold shower might be nice, Haley thought. But instead she said, "How about the Civil War?"

● ● ●

Clearly, Reese is more interested in studying Haley's anatomy than hitting the history books. What do you think prompted his further adventures? And does this mean he's ready to take their relationship to the next, more serious level?

If you think Haley wants to stick close to Reese, even if that means getting more physical (well, at least on the track), go to TRACK MEET on page 149.

Alternatively, find out what's bothering the principal *this* time around in PRINCIPAL CRUM'S LITANY on page 157.

What could be better than having the Best All Around title and the hottest guy in the sophomore class? Having all that and a track medal too.

BAND PRACTICE

All it takes is one bad note to throw off an entire performance.

Haley was sitting on the floor of Toby's finished basement, where the dark-haired drummer of the Hedon was impatiently tapping a high hat. Josh, the Hedon's lanky bassist, busied himself adjusting levels on the PA monitor, periodically looking at the wall clock and shaking his head.

Haley smoothed her newly straightened mane and tucked a lock of hair behind her ear, then shifted uncomfortably on the shag carpeting. *Where's Sasha?* she wondered, feeling like an unwelcome houseguest.

Johnny was clearly none too thrilled that Sasha was twenty minutes late to the Hedon's last rehearsal before the upcoming Battle of the Bands, and that she had invited a friend. He ignored Haley and concentrated on tuning his guitar.

Maybe this wasn't the best practice to sit in on, Haley realized.

Finally, at half past six, Sasha waltzed in, still wearing her blue warm-up suit. Her hair was up in a high ponytail, and there was a sheen on her face. It was obvious she'd come straight from a late practice.

"Sorry," she said, quickly unpacking her guitar and stepping up to the mike. "Coach kept me late running drills." No one said anything.

"Sorry ain't gonna cut it if we lose to Rubber Dynamite," Johnny said harshly.

"*Excuse* me?" Sasha said.

Haley's worst fears were being confirmed. There was serious trouble in Best Couple paradise. Sasha and Johnny had just earned that title in the class polls the day before, when Haley had shockingly been named Best All Around, ahead of both Sasha and Cecily. And now here they were fighting like a calico cat and a pit bull.

"The battle is next Saturday," Johnny said sternly. "This is *not* the practice you show up late to. Nor should it be open to . . . spectators." He glared at Haley. "Are you planning to be late on Saturday too?"

"Whatever," Sasha said. She hastily tuned her guitar and plugged in to the amplifier, then smiled apologetically at Haley. Haley figured Sasha had also neglected to tell Johnny that there was a track meet scheduled to take up most of Saturday afternoon. She sensed that the news was not going to go over well whenever Johnny finally learned the truth, probably right before the Battle of the Bands.

"One, two, three, four." Johnny counted off the tempo into the mike as Josh's deep bass line exploded out of the amp. Johnny's guitar soared over it, while Sasha more timidly eased in, laying gentle riffs over Toby's steady snare-drum beats. Sasha seemed to be keeping up until midway through the song, when Haley could tell by the look on her face that she was struggling. Then everything fell apart.

Johnny kicked over the mike and threw his guitar down. "Stop!" he yelled. "Sasha missed her cue. You're supposed to sing 'la-da-dah' after I play the 'bah-bah-bah' part."

Sasha looked on the brink of tears.

Haley adjusted her skirt restlessly. The cozy refinished basement was starting to feel way too claustrophobic. If it wouldn't have caused a further scene, she would have gotten up and gotten out. Instead, there she sat for the rest of the excruciating practice, feeling quite trapped in her little spot on the floor.

● ● ●

With the all-important Battle of the Bands only a week away, tensions are mounting. Will the Hedon be able to pull off a win, despite Sasha's missing her cues? And with Johnny acting more like a bandmate than a boyfriend, what will happen to their relationship?

If you think Haley—Ms. Best All Around—should mind her own business and not meddle in Sasha and Johnny's affairs, send her to the TRACK MEET on page 149. Alternatively, you can have Haley find out about the latest Hillsdale High "threat" eating at Principal Crum in PRINCIPAL CRUM'S LITANY on page 157.

If Sasha and Johnny split, life will go on—though it may mean the end of triple dates with Haley's friends.

PODCASTING THE POLLS

Everyone wants
to be close to a winner.

Haley was getting bombarded with text messages from Hannah Moss on the day of Dave Metzger's big podcast. She knew Dave was supposed to announce the winners of the class polls live, but she couldn't figure out why Hannah was so desperate for her to listen. *Guess she knows something I don't,* Haley thought when she received her sixth text of the day from Hannah.

Even though Haley figured her chances of winning Best All Around—the only category she was up for—were slim to none, she sat down at her laptop computer in her bedroom, clicked on the stream for "Inside Hillsdale" and tuned in just in time to catch the last of Dave's opening remarks.

"Let's go now to a word from our sponsor," Dave crooned in his newly velvety voice, which had dramatically deepened over spring break. "Hap's Diner, a casual dining establishment, family-owned since 1954, serving real food for real people daily. Did you know that Hap's is now offering gift certificates? Folks, here is the perfect way to celebrate those high points in your year, like Mother's Day, Father's Day, graduation day, Memorial Day or Independence Day. Are you in search of a token to commemorate the next Random Acts of Kindness Day? There's no better way than Hap's gift certificates! On a quest to find that ideal gift for Harriet Tubman Day, Festivus or Take-Your-Child-to-Work Day? Or what about National Tartan Day, Salvation Army Founders Day or Librarian's Day? For those and many more occasions, a gift certificate to Hap's Diner is just the thing to make the event just a little more special." He then added in rapid staccato, "Does not apply to Hap's challenges. No more than two gift certificates may be redeemed per day. Certificates expire one year after purchase."

Dave paused for a breath.

At least Annie's slacker act hasn't totally rubbed off on Dave, Haley thought. *He's still broadcasting.*

"And now, ladies and germs, without further ado," Dave continued. "Here on 'Inside Hillsdale,' you will be the first to hear the winners of this year's class polls at Hillsdale High."

There was a drumroll.

Dave first plodded through the freshmen. Haley barely recognized any of the names except for Zoe Jones, a pretty singer/songwriter/drummer with dark skin, eyes and hair who had recently been tapped by Rubber Dynamite for her musical stylings, among other things. Zoe won Most Talented, Best All Around and Most Likely to Be Famous.

Next, Dave moved on to the sophomores.

"First up, in the most stylish category . . . Best Dressed." Dave paused for effect. "The dapper winners this year are . . . Mr. Shaun Willkommen and Miss Whitney Klein!"

Haley giggled at her desk. She wondered how Whitney was going to react to being photographed with Shaun for the yearbook.

Dave went on, "For Nicest Eyes, the winners are . . . Spencer Eton and Cecily Watson," he announced smoothly, then added as an aside, "Better watch it, Ali and Drew. They may just make eyes at each other.

"Next up, Most Likely to Succeed," Dave said, pausing momentarily. "Well, this is interesting. I must first, for the record, say that these results were doubtless double and triple checked. It seems the two sophomores voted Most Likely to Succeed this year are yours truly, host of 'Inside Hillsdale,' Dave Metzger, and Hannah Moss."

Haley wondered how *that* would go over with Annie.

"For Best Couple," Dave crooned on. "Well, no surprise here. It's Sasha Lewis and Johnny Lane. Up next, we'll reveal Class Clown. I'll give you a hint: he's big and blond. Also Most Attractive, and the all-important Best All Around! But right now I want to take a moment to thank you, the listeners. We've already hit a record for the most people ever tuning in to our show tonight, folks," he announced proudly. "So not only do you think that I, Dave Metzger, am headed for greatness down the line, but you want to know what I have to say right now. And that means something. Both to me and to our sponsors. Before we return to the last of the sophomore-class winners, a brief message from our town's favorite handy-boy helper, and a longtime supporter of the broadcast, Ryan McNally."

And with that, Haley's computer kicked her off to rebuffer the stream. *Oh, no! I got bumped off,* she thought, refreshing her screen a dozen times in a futile attempt to get back on. But it was no use. The volume of traffic was too much for Dave's server. Haley had to find out twenty minutes later via text message from Hannah that she and Reese Highland had been named Best All Around. And then, somehow, it didn't seem real.

Haley knew that Hannah had overseen parts of the vote counting. She began to think that maybe the rumors were right, that the results had been rigged. But why?

Even after Reese called to congratulate her and said he hoped he'd see her at the track meet later that week, Haley felt like a fraud.

What would make Hannah risk getting into so much trouble just to make sure I was Best All Around? she wondered. *It just doesn't make any sense. Unless . . .*

● ● ●

Dave's podcast, "Inside Hillsdale," definitely had the inside scoop this time. Announcing the class polls before the school administration? Bold. Guess it's no secret who on the yearbook committee leaked the results.

But what about Hannah? Why is she suddenly so fixated on Haley? And could she have possibly tampered with the ballots? If you think Hannah's up to no good and want to INVESTIGATE, then turn to page 153. If you want to hear more about the polls and find out Principal Crum's reaction to Dave's premature announcement, go to PRINCIPAL CRUM'S LITANY on page 157. If you'd rather have Haley connect with her fellow Best All Around–er, Reese, then make a last-minute addition to the Hillsdale High track roster and send her to the TRACK MEET on page 149. Finally, instead of running laps, CHEER FOR the Best-Dressed Class Clown, SHAUN, on page 167.

Haley's newly elected to highest social rank in the class, which means everyone wants to spend time with her. Having lots of options isn't a bad thing, but it's up to you to help Haley spot the fakes.

V IS FOR VANQUISHED

Winning streaks
inevitably come to an end.

Coco De Clerq had been slaughtering her opponents on the tennis court in recent weeks. While barely breaking a sweat, she had bested the current number-one seed in the county, 6–0, 6–1. And another ranked player from Ridgewood had experienced a similar fate, ultimately breaking down and openly weeping on the court after Coco systematically dismantled her.

Given the De Clerq record, Haley assumed that the upcoming regionals would be a cinch. Especially since Coco and her coach had all the tapes Haley had been making of the matches at their disposal. The duo's rigorous hours-long daily preparation was on par with that of the pros.

Which is why it came as a total shock to see Coco so off her game—in round one, no less.

Coco was missing shots even Haley could've aced. Her ground strokes had no topspin. Her first serve had lost its usual depth and speed. And there was absolutely no evidence of all the work at the net Coco and Brad had done in her last few practices. Still, Garrett "the Troll" Noll and Chopper from the Floods kept up the cheering section, helping Coco limp along until she could eke out a win in a tiebreaker in the third set. "Go, Tigre!" they could frequently be heard calling out. Chopper, who had taken to wearing a tiger-striped cowboy hat and was calling Coco by the nickname her coach had bestowed upon her, had managed to gather the dregs of his neighborhood together to root for his new crush.

Coco's second match wasn't any prettier, and had it not been for the aging eyes of a geriatric line judge, Coco's opponent likely would have advanced rather than her.

Haley was beginning to have serious doubts about whether Coco could handle the finals in her present condition—even if the game was being played on De Clerq home turf at the Bergen County

Country Club. Brad too seemed frustrated and a little bewildered by his star player's meltdown.

With everyone wondering just what—or who—had broken Coco's concentration, Haley caught sight of Spencer Eton lurking by the clubhouse. *Uh-oh,* she thought. Coco was most definitely aware of his presence, Haley realized, noticing the familiar jaw clench.

"Hi, doll," Whitney called to Haley as she boldly climbed over the laps of several tennis fans. "I hit the pool bar for prematch treats." Whitney was carrying a large Arnold Palmer and a big bag of air-popped popcorn.

"Um, I'm okay, thanks," said Haley, somewhat surprised to see Whitney there, since Whitney was technically barred from entering the BCCC. *Guess they have to let everyone in during the regionals,* Haley realized, trying to make room for Whitney.

"Gosh, it's good to be back here," Whitney enthused. Haley saw that two club attendants were scowling in their direction.

"Cute top. Is that new?" Haley asked, admiring Whitney's pretty blue ruffled blouse. She couldn't help wondering if it was one of the spoils of Whitney's recent flirtation with shoplifting.

"I made it myself," Whitney announced, looking down at her shirt. "Do you think it makes my boobs look too big?" Haley shook her head. She was impressed. The stitching was nice, and the shirt had just the right amount of detail without looking too fussy. "If you want, I could make you one. I have this fabric in three different colors." Haley was amused.

"Don't you think Brad is sort of hot?" Whitney observed, sipping her Arnold Palmer as they stared down at Coco's coach. "If my mom wasn't moving in with Mr. Lewis, I would totally tell her to date that. Trish and my dad would *hate* it."

"Yeah. Have you heard from them at all?"

"I got a postcard last week. I think they're finally coming home, actually," said Whitney. "Ooh, do you know, Trish used to hook up with Brad, from what I hear? In the club stalls. Ew, that is so gross. For Brad, I mean. Speaking of hot and single, Johnny Lane is supposedly back on the market, or close to it."

"You're kidding," Haley said. "Hillsdale's perfect pair, Johnny Lane and Sasha Lewis, are on the *rocks*? But they're Best Couple in the sophomore class."

"I know, right? It's so iconic." Haley didn't feel like correcting her. "Sasha and Johnny get named Best Couple and then they break up, like, the next day."

I wonder what this means for the Hedon and the Battle of the Bands? Haley thought.

Whitney seemed to be reading Haley's mind. "I guess Sasha's been trying to juggle the band with running track, and Johnny wants her to choose. Of course she won't. She's too stubborn. I do know my future sister. Even if we're not speaking to each other right now."

It was a breathless moment as the best player in Hudson County gave the ball a light toss, arched her back and drew her racket back over her shoulder. *Maybe, just maybe, Coco can pull this off,* her family and friends were all thinking. But not for long. Coco's opponent paused, then released all her might in one fluid motion, sending her first ace right past the unsuspecting Coco De Clerq. From there, the bloodbath continued. Coco never led a single game, and handed over the title in just under an hour. Brad had to practically carry her off the court.

● ● ●

What an embarrassment for Coco, losing in front of the whole town like that. And this after her recent social downfall. The once-popular De Clerq wasn't even *nominated* for a single class superlative. Will this latest defeat send her over the edge?

If you can't help feeling concerned about Coco, go to page 163, COCO COMES TO HER SENSES.

If you think Haley has better things to worry about than Coco's mood and tennis swings, have her stop being a spectator and start competing: make her join the track team on page 149, TRACK MEET. Lastly, find out what Principal Crum is obsessing over this time around in PRINCIPAL CRUM'S LITANY, page 157.

THE CHEN HOUSEHOLD

Playing dress-up
is not only for girls.

When Haley was asked to Irene's house for dinner with Shaun and Devon, at first she hesitated. She'd only been to Irene's once before. Irene rarely had time off from work at the Golden Dynasty, and she never liked people to come over when her parents were home. But tonight, Irene's parents were working at the restaurant, and much to Haley's surprise, Irene had gotten the night off. The occasion was to mark what was evidently a monumental event: her grandmother was cooking.

Irene had on a black vintage dress with a red patent-leather belt when Haley arrived in her antique yellow cocktail dress. It was clear both girls had gone shopping at Jack's. Meanwhile, Irene's grandmother was ensconced in the kitchen, preparing a traditional Chinese meal. *She looks ancient,* thought Haley, noticing the rounded hunch in the elderly woman's back.

"It's like she's been over that stove for centuries," Irene said.

"Where are the boys?" asked Haley. Grandma Chen was evidently not observing Mr. Chen's strict no-dating policy.

"They—they should be here any minute," stammered Irene, almost tripping over herself as she hurried to the mirror on the wall.

Haley looked down and saw that Irene had on a pair of vintage red leather shoes with a tiny heel, but it was nevertheless a heel. *Irene wearing slingbacks?* she thought, amazed. This was their first official double date, and there was something about being dressed up in cocktail attire that had both of the girls feeling slightly goofy but giddy.

When the doorbell rang, Irene's grandma pushed past the girls on her way to open the front door. Haley heard Shaun stumbling to get out a polite greeting in Chinese, something Irene must have taught him, Haley realized. Irene's grandmother didn't say anything in return, but she nodded and let the boys in.

Shaun and Devon strutted across the wall-to-wall-carpeted living room dressed in ruffled tuxedos, also from Jack's, with carnations in their lapels.

As Irene's grandmother returned to the kitchen, Shaun and Irene embraced and furiously began making out, something they were prone to do these days. "You look . . . awesome," said Devon, awkwardly trying to ignore the other couple.

"Thanks," said Haley. "I got it at your store, as you know."

"Well, it didn't look anything like that on the rack," he commented.

Suddenly, Irene's grandmother barged back in and started yelling in Chinese and gesturing furiously. Irene assured everyone that she was just venting about the dumplings not cooking fast enough and the guests having nothing to eat. She swore the food would be ready soon.

Above the dining table, Irene had strung Chinese paper lanterns, which gave the room a soft red glow. As the foursome took their seats, Shaun couldn't keep his eyes off Irene. Haley almost felt shocked by how much attention Irene was garnering for wearing a real dress.

"The eighth wonder of the world: my girlfriend!" proclaimed Shaun.

"My father would freak out if he knew you were saying that at his dining room table," said Irene. "But I like it."

Devon reached into his pocket and took out a digital camera he'd borrowed from the school's art department. He started snapping images, recording the mood, the lighting. Finally, Irene's grandmother came into the dining room and started doling out dumplings and broth to everyone.

"De-li-cious," said Haley loudly, complimenting their chef.

"I not deaf," the old woman said in return.

"Hey, did you guys hear what happened with the class polls?" Irene announced, replenishing Shaun's empty bowl with half a ladle full. "They were totally rigged. No offense, Haley. I know you won Best All Around."

"Oh no, Shaun," mocked Devon. "Your dual honors of Most Stylish and Most Humorous Man on the Planet might be revoked."

"Drat!" Shaun bellowed. The sheer volume of his voice carried into the kitchen, causing Irene's grandmother to hobble back into the room. Grandma Chen tried to start clearing Shaun's dishes, thinking that was what he wanted.

"No! No!" said Shaun. "More! More!"

"I have an idea," Irene announced. "What do you say we ask the *I Ching* a few questions after dinner?"

"Gnihc I eht pihsrow I, dar," Shaun said backward.

"But can you handle the truth about the future?" Irene asked Shaun flirtatiously.

"From you, absolutely," Shaun replied, batting a paw at her.

Haley looked at Devon and wondered if the *I Ching* would tell her anything about her future with him.

● ● ●

How nice of Irene's grandmother to cook dinner for everyone. It was even nicer of her not to tell Mr. Chen about the secret double date night. If you are sure Haley is going to root for Shaun with Irene at the next track meet, go to page 167, CHEER FOR SHAUN. To find out more about the rigging of the class polls, turn to PRINCIPAL CRUM'S LITANY on page 157.

Irene and Shaun appear to be getting very comfortable as a couple. But is Haley feeling any closer to Devon? Hopefully, the *I Ching* will answer all her questions about life and love. That is, if you don't answer them first.

TRACK MEET

**You know it's the real thing
when he isn't turned off
by your red face and
a muddy track uniform.**

Haley sailed through the meet as if her feet didn't even need to connect with the track. She had never felt lighter or more agile, and the surge of adrenaline brought on by the competition seemed to shave seconds off each step.

Maybe it had something to do with the fact that she and Reese were on the same team. Each time she rounded a turn and faced the bleachers, she could see him standing on the bench, cheering her on.

Or maybe it was just because Haley was learning that she liked to compete. She liked pulling away from the others as they struggled and faltered at her back. She liked the look on Coach Tygert's face when she took yet another top place or second. And she loved the admiration and frustration that flashed across her opponents' faces once she had crossed the finish line ahead of them.

In fact, the only thing Haley didn't like about her first official track meet was besting Sasha in nearly every event.

Sasha was, to put it mildly, off her stride. Usually she was explosive in short distance races, but in the 50-meter dash she had tripped on a shoelace. Her longer times, once consistent, were now all over the place, and she had finished dead last in the 5,000-meter.

"You okay?" Haley asked her friend between the 400-meter and the 110-meter hurdles.

Sasha yawned and said, "Yeah, I'm just tired." But Haley knew it was more than that. For starters, Johnny wasn't sitting in the home team cheering section. And Sasha hadn't exactly rocked at her last few band practices. Maybe doing both track and the Hedon, though possible, was *im*possible to do really *well*.

"Sash, it's only a bad day. We all have them," Reese said, patting her on the back. "Don't think about it. Just run."

Sasha smiled weakly. "Thanks," she said. "By the way, are you guys coming to the Battle of the Bands tonight? I know how tired you can be after a race."

"Are you kidding?" Reese said. "We've only rallied together a huge cheering section. You know you can count on us."

"Let's go Shau-nee!" Irene Chen yelled at that moment from the green. She was wearing a gold lamé prom dress over jeans and had gold stripes on her cheeks. Her hair was also dyed with bright blue streaks, and she seemed to have stolen a set of pompoms from the Hawks' cheerleading team.

Sitting next to Irene was Devon McKnight, the hot photographer who always seemed to be eyeing Haley—in the halls at school, in the parking lot after class and now, out on the track field. Haley stretched for a moment and listened to their conversation.

"Sucks you can't go to the Battle of the Bands tonight," said Irene.

"I know," said Devon. "But I've got to watch my kid sister. I don't think my parents would take too kindly to me bringing her to a rock concert."

"It's a catch-22," said Irene. "You need a girlfriend to hang out with on all those nights you get stuck babysitting. But you can't get a girlfriend because you're always stuck at home—"

"Babysitting," they said in unison.

"It's rotten luck, man," Irene added.

Haley thought so too.

• • •

Poor Devon. Always stuck at home watching his kid sister. That's clearly the only explanation for why such a hottie doesn't already have a steady love interest.

Could Haley be curious about Devon, even though she's currently steady with Reese? Is it possible to like two people at the same time? Or does everyone have only one true soul mate? And if so, who is Haley's perfect match?

If you think Reese is her destiny, send her to THE BATTLE OF THE BANDS on page 172.

If you think the brooding photographer is more her speed, have Haley BABYSIT WITH DEVON on page 215.

Finally, if you think this is all too confusing and want Haley to go spend some time at home to regroup and see how she really feels, have her EDIT HOME MOVIES WITH DAD on page 211.

Sins of omission often constitute a crime.

Haley couldn't stop thinking about the guilty look she'd seen on Hannah Moss's face earlier that day. *What could she be up to?* Haley wondered, suspecting it might have something to do with the yearbook polls.

Then there was the fact that Haley just didn't believe that she had won the Best All Around category for the sophomore class fair and square. *It's my first year here,* she thought. *Why would anyone vote for me? There's no way I beat out* both *Sasha and Cecily.*

There were rumors the results had been fixed,

and Haley's instinct was that Hannah had been the one doing the tampering. So when Hannah and her closely guarded book bag exited the school through the back doors that afternoon, Haley began tailing her with her video camera, staying just far enough behind that she wouldn't be detected.

Whatever's in that bag of hers, I'm going to find out, Haley thought, noticing that Hannah did seem a little paranoid. Ms. Moss kept looking over her shoulder as she walked out behind the school and into the side parking lot, toward a big row of Dumpsters.

Haley hid behind a parked car to stake out the scene from a safe distance. Unfortunately, the car belonged to one of the senior English teachers, who soon arrived and stood over Haley impatiently, looking as though he was anxious to leave for the day. "Ahem," he said deliberately, forcing Haley to skulk over to the next car. The teacher then got into his coupe and drove off, momentarily spooking Hannah. Haley thought she'd lost her for good, but then Hannah reappeared from behind one of the Dumpsters. Haley hit Record, documenting Hannah's every move through the zoom lens.

First, Hannah took handful after handful of crumpled papers out of her bag. Then she began tossing them into the Dumpster. Haley zoomed in even closer. She was hoping to make out any text on the pages, but it was difficult. *Obviously getting rid of the evidence!* Haley guessed.

After Hannah finished emptying her bag, she looked around furtively, then walked quickly across the parking lot to meet a cab that was waiting for her at the entrance to the school. Hannah was forever taking cabs, Haley knew, because her parents refused to let her ride the bus, and their work schedules prevented them from dropping her off and picking her up each day. They were both busy physicists. Haley had heard that Mr. and Mrs. Moss had once offered to get Hannah a full-time driver, but Hannah had turned them down, fearing such an arrangement was "conspicuous."

If I had the chance at a full-time chauffeur, no way would I give that up, Haley thought.

The cab exited the parking lot as Haley made her way over to the Dumpsters. She pulled out some of the papers Hannah had tossed, and sure enough . . . they were sophomore-class poll sheets.

Haley sighed and shook her head, no longer simply concerned that the polls had been rigged. She felt sure she had just gathered the evidence to prove it. But what should she do with the footage and the discarded sheets? *I can't believe Hannah would really do this,* Haley kept thinking, recalling the widespread perception of Hannah Moss as a brainy, harmless wunderkind. Hannah had, after all, just been named Most Likely to Succeed. Though of course, Haley realized, she could've rigged that category too. *Hannah has seemed left out ever since spring break.*

Annie and Dave barely talk to her anymore. Maybe she was just trying to impress everyone?

The other complicating factor was the yearbook schedule. Haley knew if she went public with her findings, Principal Crum would demand that the proofs be recalled from the printer, and then every single one of the polls would need to be rechecked to verify the results. That could mean the school might end up without a yearbook this year.

How could I do that to everyone, especially the seniors? she thought. *But then, how can I let the sophomore superlatives stand, knowing that more deserving people than me should have won?*

Haley had no idea what to do.

● ● ●

It seems Haley is in the hot seat. Does having the evidence mean it's her moral duty to turn Hannah in? What if there's more to the story than meets the eye?

If Haley decides to take what she saw at face value, have her BLAME HANNAH on page 184. Alternatively, if you think Haley doesn't want to ruin Hannah's life but still has a responsibility to her student body to at least demand a RECOUNT, turn to page 180.

A little additional questioning might help Haley get to the bottom of this incident. Unfortunately, there's no more time.

PRINCIPAL CRUM'S LITANY

The voice of the people can't be heard if the election results get monkeyed with.

Principal Crum was furious that the class poll results had been prematurely announced on Dave Metzger's podcast. He had not personally authorized that release of "sensitive" and "classified" Hillsdale High documents. There were also widespread reports of possible vote tampering, which caused him to issue a schoolwide chartreuse alert and immediately call an assembly.

Haley crammed into the packed bleachers along with the rest of her homeroom class. There wasn't an inch between her and Annie Armstrong, even with Annie practically sitting on Dave's lap.

"Look, just play it cool," Annie said to Dave casually. Haley saw that Dave's hives were beginning to resurface. He had broken out in red blotches on his face and neck, worried that Principal Crum might publicly press him for answers on just how he came across the results. "You didn't do anything *illegal,* per se."

"You're right," Dave agreed, loosening his collar. "This is, after all, the information age. I, as a journalist, have an obligation to share news with the public."

"Besides, Crum's latest litany will be great advertising for the podcast," Annie reminded him.

Where's Hannah? Haley wondered, realizing the pixieish Ms. Moss was not among the crowd. *That's strange. She never misses school.*

Haley tried to slide down the bench to free up some space, but Chopper and the Troll were dominating the area to her left. They kept unsuccessfully trying to start the wave. Both outcasts had *Go, Coco!* fake tattoos emblazoned on their foreheads, while Chopper had recently shaved his head into a sort of Mohawk, with the remaining hair shaped into a giant *C.*

I wonder how Coco feels about her new cheering section, Haley thought. But then, after Coco's embarrassing social downfall a few months back, who else was going to show up at her tennis matches and root for her?

With a scowl on his face, Principal Crum marched up to the podium. He cleared his throat, only to begin coughing uncontrollably into the microphone, prompting his secretary to dash over with a mug of water.

"Ahem," Crum began. "Students of Hillsdale, I regret to inform you that the results of the class polls you might have heard last night at eight p.m. on Dave Metzger's podcast, 'Inside Hillsdale,' were not valid."

The crowd began to hoot and holler savagely.

"In fact," Crum continued in spite of the racket, "the administration has reason to suspect that this year's class polls were *rigged*." The students were now openly booing. Principal Crum pounded his fist on the podium. "Listen up, people! This is serious! How will we know for sure if Debbie Garfield and Richie Huber are the real Class Clowns of the senior class if we don't verify these results?"

At that moment, Richie let out a loud fart that ricocheted off the walls. "That was not funny!" Crum shouted, though you could barely hear him over all the laughter. "Order!" He picked up his gavel this time and rapped it hard on the podium. "Now. There is worrisome evidence to support these claims. Mr. Gunter, the night attendant, found stacks of used ballots in the parking lot Dumpsters. Why he was searching the Dumpsters is another story, but I digress. Willy, one of our valued bus drivers, who, by the way, is retiring next month—Louise, did you ever order that cake?—located other discarded ballots on some of the buses."

Just then, a paper airplane launched somewhere in the nosebleed seats floated down gracefully, circling the air around Principal Crum's head before it finally landed smoothly on the freshly waxed gymnasium floor. Principal Crum crushed the plane underfoot.

"Given these unsettling developments, I'm considering calling for an immediate recount. That will mean each of you will have to check in with your homeroom teachers and verify whom you voted for, a process that could take days or even weeks and may culminate with our having no polls at all this year." The boos returned with a vengeance. "Since we believe the culprit may in some way be involved with the yearbook committee, we're also going to pull the proofs of the entire yearbook from the printer. We will be checking and rechecking everything else in its pages, to make certain this is an isolated instance of academic sabotage. Let's just hope there's enough time to resubmit. Otherwise, Hillsdale High might be without a yearbook this year." The crowd booed. "Now, now, I know you're all as outraged and upset as I am, but this regrettable scenario might just be avoided if the unethical person or persons who discarded these crucial ballots steps forward at once to explain himself or herself. I promise, there will be no undue punishment or stigma attached if you turn yourself in."

"Did someone say . . . SIGMA?" a voice yelled out in the stands. "Pool party at Richie's this weekend! No password necessary!" This triggered an eruption of cheers.

"People, did you not even hear what I just said?" Crum responded sternly into the mike. "If no one steps forward to admit his or her involvement in the rigging of the class polls, then we're looking at a *Talon*-less year," he threatened once again. "Don't you understand what that means? Have you no sense of history? Of capturing these precious moments of your high school years in a handsome, faux leather–bound volume with glossy, expensive stock, which sells for twenty-seven dollars and which you can pass around to all your friends, teachers and classmates to sign with sometimes-amusing but mostly banal reminiscences of your time here together?"

"Who wants to pay thirty bucks for a scrapbook? Last year's *Talon* sucked!" someone yelled.

Principal Crum looked disgusted. "Dismissed," he said bitterly. And with that, Hillsdale High's ranking officer stormed off in the direction of the teachers' lounge.

• • •

When isn't Principal Crum on the warpath? What is it about school rules and law enforcement that gets him so jazzed?

If you think it's Haley's responsibility to look into the problems with the polls, have her oversee the RE-COUNT on page 180.

If you think Haley is positive that Hannah Moss was the one who tampered with the tally, have her go tell Principal Crum what she suspects and BLAME HAN-NAH on page 184 in order to save the yearbook.

With the seniors preparing to graduate, check out the wildest pool party of the year at Richie's pad on page 205, SENIOR SIGMA.

Choosing between saving the school yearbook and going to the biggest senior pool party in the history of Hillsdale shouldn't be any trouble at all.

COCO COMES
TO HER SENSES

**The tighter someone's wound,
the more likely they are
to snap.**

Haley sat on the floor of Coco's bedroom, at a loss over what to do. Coco was staring catatonically out her window. She hadn't eaten, slept or spoken a single word since losing her final match at the regionals, a full two days prior. Nor had she even bothered to change out of her sweaty, clay-smeared tennis whites.

"Coco?" Haley said tentatively for the umpteenth time. "Why don't you try some of this consommé Consuela fixed for you?" No response. "Do you want one of the cookies your mom baked?" Again, nothing. "Your mom must really care about you. I don't think I've ever seen her in an apron before. And Consuela said it's practically the first time that oven has ever been used."

Coco persisted in gazing blankly ahead. Her posture was, as ever, perfectly erect. Haley was beginning to wonder if maybe someone shouldn't call a doctor.

"Here, let's get you some fresh air," Haley offered, stepping into Coco's line of sight to open the window. *Anything to snap her out of it,* she thought, lifting the double-hung window. Haley paused. She heard the faint sound of music coming from somewhere below. At first, she thought it must have been Jorge, the groundskeeper, playing music while he trimmed the hedges or cleaned the pool. But then it grew louder. And louder. And louder.

Finally, Chopper, still in the same clothes *he* had been wearing at the tennis match and still sporting his *C*-shaped Mohawk, emerged from the shrubbery holding up a rather large boom box and blasting "In Your Eyes" by Peter Gabriel.

The Troll popped out of the bushes next, following a few paces behind. He brushed off a few leaves and looked up at Haley. "You know, he hasn't spoken or eaten in two days," the Troll said in a disapproving tone while pointing at Chopper. "Even though I told him we're about to miss the Battle of the Bands."

"Has he been out here this whole time?" Haley asked.

"Yep," the Troll said, then added, practically screaming in Chopper's ear, "Someone should talk some sense into him."

"Tell me about it," said Haley, glancing back over her shoulder at Coco.

Chopper just turned up the volume on the boom box. Haley was about to return to tending her charge when Coco stirred.

"Come on, turn it off, man," the Troll yelled at Chopper down on the lawn. "No chick is worth debasing yourself like this. Grow a spine."

The Troll tried to yank the boom box out of his hands. They struggled. Then Haley called down to them, "Wait!" She held her breath as Coco rose and walked—shuffled was more like it—over to the window. Chopper held the boom box up even higher, then glared at the Troll as if to say, *See. It's* working.

Coco, weak and exhausted, peered down at them with sunken, hollow eyes, then lifted her arms, grabbed hold of the window and slammed it shut.

She began to shuffle slowly back toward the bed, and Haley stepped out of her way. As Coco sat back down, Haley held out the consommé, and this time, Coco accepted it. She took two sips, then said, "I need to see Ali." She took another sip, then added, "And Spencer."

"I think they're at Richie's house, for senior

SIGMA," Haley replied. "You probably wouldn't want to go there . . . like this." Coco stared at her, her eyes boring into Haley's. Haley was terrified of that gaze. "I mean, let's go. Why not?" Haley said, conceding. "But first you have to finish your soup."

● ● ●

Chopper must have felt pretty bad when Coco slammed her window shut. Maybe Coco should be more polite to her suitors. After all, Chopper's the *only* boy at school paying any attention to her these days.

To accompany Coco to SENIOR SIGMA as she tracks down Ali and Spencer, turn to page 205.

If you think Coco's out of the woods and can handle things on her own from here, and you would rather see Haley go to THE BATTLE OF THE BANDS, turn to page 172.

Things in Coco's life tend to be all or nothing lately. So it should be interesting to see how Ali and Spencer respond to her next move.

CHEER FOR SHAUN

Agility doesn't necessarily correspond to weight.

"**G**o Shau-nee!" Irene yelled, waving the pair of blue pom-poms she had stolen from the Hillsdale High JV cheerleading squad earlier that afternoon. Irene was wearing a loose-fitting gold lamé prom dress over jeans, in honor of the big track meet, and she had painted gold stripes just below her eyes. Haley noticed that her friend had also dyed several chunks of her hair bright blue, an irreverent touch that completed Irene the artist's interpretation of school spirit.

Shaun, who was out on the field warming up, stopped midstretch and blew Irene a kiss. He was wearing a blue terry headband, gold aviator sunglasses, a white tank top with his number, 77, hand-painted on the front and back, a pair of royal blue vintage men's short shorts—which he had picked up at Jack's during one of Devon's shifts—white knee socks with blue stripes around the calves and blue running shoes that looked straight out of 1978. "This is for you, baby," Shaun yelled, looking at Irene and pointing toward the hurdles.

"Wow, do you really think he can jump that high?" Haley asked Devon, who was sitting next to her on the lawn, his cheeks already starting to turn a golden brown in the sun. They stared at the waist-high hurdles, then at Shaun's massive love handles and his thighs bulging out of his tight shorts.

"I don't know," said Devon, shaking his head. "That's a lot of meat to move over that spit."

"Come on, people, positive thoughts," Irene said, closing her eyes.

Haley shrugged, took a yoga pose and said, "Ohmmmmm."

"Just concentrate on Shaun making it over each jump," Irene instructed.

Haley opened one eye, glanced at Devon and whispered, "The visual is a lot like counting sheep. Really, really plump sheep." Devon laughed.

"I heard that," Irene said, scowling.

Out of her one open eye, Haley caught sight of Sasha Lewis sitting on the Hawks bench, looking distraught. "What's up with the golden girl?" Haley asked Irene.

"From what I hear, there's trouble on Lover's Lane," Irene said. "Sasha's been trying to juggle track with the Hedon, and Johnny thinks she's bringing down the band."

"Do you think they'll break up?" Haley asked.

"I don't know," said Irene.

What Haley really wanted to ask her was *Do you want them to?* Irene's huge crush on Johnny hadn't exactly been a secret this year, although Irene hadn't mentioned his name in weeks.

"Hey," Devon said, changing the subject, "I have to watch my kid sister this Saturday. Why don't we take her and Mitchell to the zoo?"

"Sure," Haley said, biting her lip as he gave her a smile. Devon was cute, but he was *reeaallly* cute when he smiled, which unfortunately for Haley wasn't all that often. She watched as he brushed his blondish brown locks away from his face.

"Hey, Haley," a voice called out. Haley looked up to see Reese Highland jogging by. Out of surprise, or maybe more out of habit, she blushed—a reaction Devon immediately noticed, causing the smile to disappear from his face. "You coming to the Battle of the Bands on Saturday?" Reese asked Haley. "Sasha and Johnny need our votes."

"I, um . . . we'll see" was all Haley could manage. "Good luck!" Haley called out as Reese ran over to join the rest of the track team.

Devon just shook his head. "Guess that means the zoo is out," he said sarcastically. "What girl could resist the Natural Highland?"

Haley felt terrible. It wasn't as if Reese was really a threat to her relationship with Devon. Or was he? Why did she always get so nervous whenever Reese Highland came around? And would there ever be a time when Devon would feel secure with her and not get jealous of her friendly neighbor?

The referee called the runners to the starting line, and Haley picked up her video camera. She had lately taken to recording all the eventful moments in her friends' lives, as a way of documenting her first year of living in New Jersey. But right now, she was just grateful to have the camcorder to hide behind, at least until she figured out what she was going to do.

● ● ●

Um, can you say *awkward*? How's Haley ever supposed to decide between Devon and Reese if they both always seem to ask her out at exactly the same time?

What do you think she should do? Is it possible to like two people at the same time? Or does everyone have only one true soul mate? And if so, who is Haley's perfect match?

If you think she should be with Reese, send her to **THE BATTLE OF THE BANDS** on page 172.

If you think the brooding photographer is more her speed, send her to **BABYSIT WITH DEVON** on page 215.

Finally, if you think this is all too confusing and want Haley to go spend some time at home to regroup and see how she really feels, have her **EDIT HOME MOVIES WITH DAD** on page 211.

THE BATTLE OF THE BANDS

Even the crowd favorite can choke.

"This is going to be a close one tonight," Reese said as he stood in line in front of the community amphitheater on Saturday night, along with Haley, Cecily and Drew.

"I know! I almost don't want to watch," Cecily agreed nervously. They all were anxiously awaiting entry into the Battle of the Bands, where the Hedon, Rubber Dynamite and other local rockers were about to compete for the title of Bergen County Band of the Year.

"That was an intense track meet this morning," Cecily said, rubbing her tight hamstrings. "I just don't know how Sasha is going to have the energy to perform after all that."

"Oh, she'll be fine," said Reese. But just as the words left his mouth, his face stretched into a gigantic yawn.

"My point exactly," said Cecily.

They handed the door person their tickets and walked in. The amphitheater was swarming with kids from all the local public and private schools. Haley felt almost as put off as she had on her first day at Hillsdale High. *At least I have Reese, Cecily and Drew,* she thought, holding on for dear life to her cute neighbor's arm, lest she get lost in the crowd.

Everyone seemed to be pushing toward the stage, trying to get the best view possible. "This is a mess," said Cecily as two oafs from Ridgewood rudely shoved past her. "You know, you can't even hear anything when you're that close to the speakers," she called after them.

"My ears are already ringing," Reese admitted, cringing at the thrash band that had just started playing. "Here, I know where we should go." He took Haley by the hand; she held on to Cecily, Cecily grabbed Drew, and they made their way through the writhing horde. Reese led them behind a sturdy gazebo on the edge of the park. He waited until the security guards weren't watching, then hoisted

Haley up to the roof. Cecily was next, then Drew gave Reese a boost and climbed up on his own. Sitting atop the gazebo, they had a perfect view of the stage and were just far enough from the speakers to hear the music without having to shout to carry on a conversation. "Much better," said Reese.

Haley looked at the dance pit just in time to see Shaun Willkommen, still in his track uniform, though now also wearing a gold cape, launch himself off the stage. He landed right on top of a group of Hillsdale High football players, who passed him along overhead, allowing him to surf the crowd.

That certainly would not have been possible a few months ago, before Shaun lost twenty pounds and joined the track team, Haley thought. *He must be so psyched about placing third in the hurdles today.*

"That kid is nuts," said Drew, shaking his head at their new teammate. Shaun continued riding the crowd's outstretched arms until a girl tried to support his weight and couldn't quite do it. She began to cave, which sent Shaun crashing to the ground. But within seconds, he'd popped back up, looking pumped and ready to ride again.

After the thrash band finished its set, there was a short pause before the next act assumed position onstage. Haley knew instantly from the three keyboards being set up that Rubber Dynamite was about to play. Sure enough, moments later, the band's trio of mysteriously jumpsuited and masked keyboardists materialized. Only this time, they had with them a new girl, a very pretty member of the Hillsdale High freshman class named Zoe Jones. She had dark, coffee-colored skin, eyes and hair, and was dressed in a white denim miniskirt with a hot pink off-the-shoulder T-shirt, not quite in keeping with the rest of the band. But they were smart to capitalize on her looks for crowd appeal. All the guys in the mosh pit were transfixed.

Zoe sat down behind a drum kit in the center of the stage, took a moment to collect herself, then began softly tapping the high hat with what looked to be a pair of wire kitchen whisks. With her left hand, she played a set of chimes stationed next to the drum kit. The eerie whine of the keyboards was soon layered over Zoe's percussive foundation, and finally Zoe and one of the Rubber Dynamite guys began a haunting duet.

"Wow. Okay, Sasha's really in trouble," said Drew, articulating what everyone else on the roof was thinking. Zoe had an unusual but highly appealing voice that always seemed to hover on the edge of a pitch, threatening to fall out but somehow managing to hang on.

"She's *really* good," Reese said, which made Haley feel the slightest bit jealous.

Moments later, Cecily pointed out Annie Armstrong and Dave Metzger canoodling in the front row. They were both barefoot, and Annie had on a long white cotton off-the-shoulder dress, while Dave was wearing what looked to be white cotton pajamas. "Can you believe those two?" Cecily asked. "Because of them, we might not have a yearbook this year. And they've got the nerve to blow off yet another *Talon* deadline and come here tonight? That's so lame."

"Half the proofs aren't in," Drew added, "and it may be too late to get anything else to the printer. Plus, someone's evidently rigged the polls, so Principal Crum is threatening no *Talon* this year."

"But he can't do that!" Haley exclaimed. "This is my first year in Hillsdale, and you're telling me I might not get a freaking yearbook to commemorate it?"

"Imagine how the seniors feel," Reese said.

"I'm afraid Crum can and will," Cecily warned. "In fact, he might even *enjoy* punishing the whole school like that, to remind everyone of how much power he has over us."

A little while later, the murmur of voices throughout the amphitheater formed into a cohesive chant as the final band prepared to take the stage. "He-don! He-don! He-don!" the kids roared in feverish anticipation. The stage lights rose to reveal Sasha, Johnny, Josh and Toby silhouetted on the bandshell. A bass guitar ripped forth, followed by the wail of Sasha's and Johnny's guitars. Their voices intertwined, climbing above the propulsive beat Toby was providing on the tom-toms.

It was a commanding introduction, and the crowd erupted accordingly. However, the moment was not to last. It was hard to pinpoint exactly when the band lost its unity, but somewhere in the middle of the second song, the tempo fell off, and then Sasha flubbed the lyrics and skipped ahead to play the refrain while everyone else was still in the middle of a verse. Realizing they were off, Johnny tried valiantly to hold them all together, but it was no use. Josh and Toby soon fell out of step, and the crowd picked up on their mistakes and unleashed a torrent of boos.

"That's harsh," said Haley, wincing at the mob's reaction. Reese nodded in agreement, and Cecily cast a worried look at Haley. They all knew what this meant: the Hedon was not going to walk away with the title of Bergen County Band of the Year. And what would that mean for Sasha and Johnny?

Haley, Reese, Cecily and Drew filled out their ballots, voting of course for the Hedon. But Rubber Dynamite with special guest Zoe Jones still won handily.

Haley and her friends waited in the parking lot as the Hedon members slowly trickled out, looking beyond forlorn. Haley spotted Sasha and Johnny first. They were carrying their equipment and didn't seem to be speaking to each other.

"Good effort, guys!" Cecily called over.

"You'll get 'em next year," Haley added, but Johnny scoffed. Reese, Haley and Drew clapped supportively, but nothing seemed to be cheering up the unhappy couple.

"Hey, we're going to Hap's," Reese said, adding, "Haley and I still have those gift certificates we won on field day. Wanna join us? Our treat."

"Sounds like fun," Sasha said feebly. Her voice was painfully hoarse.

Johnny, on the other hand, wasn't speaking at all. Nor was he looking at Sasha. After he finished loading his stuff into the trunk of Toby's car, he got into the passenger seat without saying goodbye and without checking into Sasha's plans for the night.

"Actually, I'm pretty beat," Sasha said, staring guiltily at Johnny. She turned to Haley and Reese and forced a smile. "Maybe I should just plan on seeing you guys at school next week?" Sasha climbed into the backseat, leaned her head against the window and closed her eyes.

Haley didn't know if Sasha and Johnny as a couple would even make it through the night, but she knew their fate would likely hinge on what was said in the next couple of hours.

● ● ●

Fine, the Hedon didn't win the battle against Zoe Jones and Rubber Dynamite. But getting booed by the

audience? That bruised some egos. No wonder Johnny Lane is all bent out of shape. Unfortunately, there's nothing Haley can do for Sasha and Johnny now except wait.

If you think Haley would never miss a trip to Hap's Diner with Reese, go to page 198, FREE MEAL AT HAP'S. If you are horrified by the possibility of there being no yearbook this year, find out the latest news on that front and maybe offer a little help on page 219, ANNIE COMES TO HER SENSES.

No yearbook, or no more Best Couple? Neither possibility seems all that appealing.

Torture isn't always necessary to get answers.

Haley was convinced that Hannah Moss was behind the recent ballot tampering at Hillsdale High, so she decided to confront her face to face. After waiting for Hannah outside her fifth-period class, she briskly escorted her into the closest ladies' room for an interrogation.

"Do you have something you want to tell me?" Haley demanded.

There was an awkward silence as the girls stared at each other.

"I saw you throw ballots in the Dumpsters out back," Haley said in an accusatory tone.

"Yeah, I threw out a whole stack of ballots," Hannah confessed readily.

Haley was confused. "So you admit it?" Haley continued. "But *why*?"

"Haley, the ballots I disposed of were all forged. Someone printed up stacks and stacks of fakes and filled them out using bogus names."

"Huh?" Haley asked, certainly not expecting *that* answer. "So you actually *prevented* the election from being rigged? That means the results Dave announced are one hundred percent accurate."

Hannah shrugged. "Well, not a hundred percent." Haley frowned.

"The results should be ninety-nine-point-one-three-five percent accurate, assuming a slight margin for human error."

Haley sighed. "Who do you think printed up the fakes?" she asked, bewildered.

"Well, I can't say for sure. But considering Coco was a write-in candidate in every major category, my guess would be Chopper or the Troll."

"Ah. . . . They are her biggest fans," Haley agreed. Just then, she noticed a flyer on the bathroom wall for a trunk show put on by Whitney Klein, Ms. Best Dressed of the sophomore class. *Whitney's designing clothes now?* Haley wondered, momentarily distracted. *Well, at least she's no longer shoplifting.*

Haley still couldn't believe Hannah had actually saved the day, no thanks to her. The entire yearbook could have been canceled if Haley had gone to Principal Crum prematurely. "Thanks for being straight with me," she said, patting the petite Hannah on the back. "Though I kinda wish you'd told me."

"I figured you had enough on your plate."

Just then, Annie Armstrong came into the restroom, looking agitated. "Hi, girls," said Annie. "Would you two have any interest in studying together next week?" Annie didn't just look agitated, Haley realized. She looked downright desperate. "Dave and I don't seem to have many, uh, notes from, oh, the last couple weeks."

"Sure," Hannah responded quickly, seemingly overjoyed to be back in the Annie-Dave fold. "You guys can copy my notes, no problem. What night works best for you?"

● ● ●

Another seriously close call. Haley almost falsely accused Hannah Moss of rigging the elections! Good thing she confronted her first. Otherwise, there might not have been a yearbook this year. Plus, Crum never would have bought Hannah's story about forged ballots. She might have been thrown out of school!

If you think Haley should stay on the straight and narrow, send her to study with her friends in ANNIE

COMES TO HER SENSES on page 219. Alternatively, go check out WHITNEY'S TRUNK SHOW on page 187.

Do you think Annie deserves Haley's help after she and Dave slacked off for half the semester? Maybe not. But a friend in need is a friend you can exploit later.

BLAME HANNAH

Playing the blame game
is never productive.

Once Haley set foot in Principal Crum's office, she felt a sharp pang of guilt. It was sheer torture to think about handing the sweet, harmless, tiny Hannah Moss over to the authorities. Haley knew it was a harsh call. But as she sat in the waiting room, she convinced herself that it was her responsibility. Really, she had no other choice. Or did she?

"Thanks for coming in, Miss Miller," Principal Crum said, welcoming Haley into his sizeable, air-conditioned office.

Haley, unable to verbally sell Hannah out, simply played the video footage she'd captured of Hannah dumping ballots into the Dumpsters. After viewing the hard evidence, Principal Crum thanked Haley again for being "a model student and citizen." He then reached into the top drawer of his desk and handed her a gift certificate to Hap's Diner, as the school paper's photographer appeared out of nowhere to capture the photo op. Haley felt gross.

The following day, without further warning, Principal Crum announced that there would not be a *Talon* yearbook that year. Haley was horrified. *What have I done? Crum said if we turned in the guilty party, it would save the yearbook from being canceled, not drive it further into the ground!* Haley quickly realized he'd only made that statement to get the culprit or an informant to step forward. She had walked right into his trap. *I'll just bet he's saving a fortune on printing fees,* she thought, irked by Principal Crum's skullduggery.

She wasn't the only one. During the next week, the senior class was in an uproar.

When the school authorities finally caught up with Hannah, she told her side of the story. Much to Haley's horror and dismay, Hannah claimed she hadn't rigged the polls at all. She was only trying to undo the damage Chopper had caused by printing up fake ballots and using false names to vote for Coco in every category. Of course no one believed her—even when she produced some of the forgeries. She was suspended, which went on her permanent record and definitely affected that future success she was voted most likely to achieve.

Hang your head and go back to page 1.

WHITNEY'S TRUNK SHOW

Crazy, mysterious, fanciful things lurk inside trunks.

On the morning of Whitney's big trunk show, Haley picked a handful of flowers from the Millers' back garden and made a bouquet to congratulate her friend on the launch of her new clothing line, WK. Whitney's father had just breezed back into town after a lengthy sojourn in the Caribbean with his much younger paramour, Trish.

Haley could tell as she walked up to the front door of the Kleins' palatial homestead that the soon-to-be-stepmonster had definitely been involved in throwing the event. *Tacky* didn't even begin to describe it. There were lime green Lunch Bunch catering trucks parked all the way out to the street, gold helium balloons tied to the handrails of the front porch and a garish purple tent erected in the side yard, where Mr. Klein was holding court amid a group of seemingly enthralled middle-aged men. Clearly, Jerry Klein had strong-armed his every friend in New Jersey into bringing their girlfriends, daughters and wives to fork over cash to his talented little "Whittles."

I hope Whitney realizes he's just trying to buy his way back into her affections, Haley thought. *What am I saying? He's totally speaking her language!*

"The trunk show is on the second floor, down the hallway on your right," a woman in a maid's uniform instructed Haley at the door.

From the smile on Whitney's face as Haley entered the makeshift showroom, Haley knew things were going well. There was Coco De Clerq, flipping through the clothing racks with all three generations of De Clerq women at her side: Ali, Mrs. D and Coco's grandmother, Starla, who was in town for Ali's graduation, and who, Haley couldn't help noticing, had bright pink lipstick smeared on her teeth. "What do you think about this for my graduation brunch?" Ali asked, holding up a little turquoise number.

"If I had your legs, I'd live in it," Starla said in a

husky voice before she went back to picking through the racks. Between the four of them, Haley figured the De Clerq women alone could afford to set Whitney up in business for life.

Haley was certainly glad to see Coco and Ali getting along again, especially since it meant that they would likely all get to spend the summer riding around in Ali's convertible. Her bag was vibrating, so she reached in and fished out her cell phone. *Annie Armstrong,* Haley thought, looking down at the caller ID. *Wonder what she wants. Probably to crib my notes for finals, now that those exams are counting for so much of our year-end grades.* She tossed the phone back into her bag without answering.

Country club regulars had also come out to the WK trunk show in droves, forming a swirl of pastels, with tennis bags slung over their shoulders. "Can I get y'all some lemonade?" Trish asked, clearly trying to impress the very same women she had formerly served as a waitress at the BCCC. Not that they were about to open their social circle to her. The women looked Trish up and down dismissively before offering a round of polite "No thank you's," then just continued shopping.

I guess men aren't allowed upstairs for a good reason, realized Haley, seeing a middle-aged woman standing in front of a mirror blatantly stripping down to try on a few of Whitney's designs. *Ew, I so did not need to see that,* Haley thought, turning away from the woman's wrinkly jelly rolls. *I hope I never get old.*

Whitney, meanwhile, was busy writing down orders at her desk. Haley came up behind her and handed her the homegrown bouquet. "Wow, thanks," Whitney said, seeming slightly flustered by the crowd. Haley saw from Whitney's expression that her friend was also having trouble doing math in her head while keeping the three women in front of her happy as they not-so-patiently waited for their orders to be recorded.

"Um, you know, that top you're getting goes perfectly with the green skort in the look book on page three," Haley offered, jumping in to save Whitney just as she was about to lose a customer. "The Quoguey Bottoms. Here, let me show you. They're sooo versatile. And on your figure . . ."

Whitney smiled at Haley, as if to say thank you. Together, they fielded questions about the look book and went on a selling spree for over two hours. When Haley and Whitney finally looked up, they had sold out the line and had enough orders to keep Whitney busy all summer.

"So, Haley, a little drunken birdie tells me that Richie Huber wants to ask you to prom," Ali said just as things were winding down.

"That vulture?" said Haley, dismissing the thought. Although she secretly couldn't help wondering what it would be like to go.

"What are you scoffing at, Coco?" Ali said, turning to her sister. "There are two senior football players who should be calling you and Whitney any minute."

"Ooh, ooh, ooh, can we go? Can we go?" Whitney begged. "I've got the perfect dresses for all of us to wear."

"I suppose it would serve those vultures right if we went and proved once and for all that underclassmen are not easy," said Coco.

"And we would look pretty great dissing them in original WK designs," Haley offered.

"So it's settled, then?" Ali said. "You guys can all come with me and Spencer. Oh, don't look so pouty, Coco. It's not a real date. I just wouldn't be caught dead with one of those vultures in my class."

The trio of sophomores looked at her and frowned.

"Kidding!" said Ali. "You girls really need to lighten up."

● ● ●

The De Clerq sister act is back in business. But what did you think of Ali's plan to send three young sophomores off to the prom with a pack of senior vultures? Should they really risk getting seriously groped just so they can wear Whitney's evening gowns and hang out with Ali and Spencer? If you think so, send Haley to PROM on page 227. God help her.

If you're more concerned about Haley's grades, send her to CRAM FOR FINALS on page 223.

There's not much time left in the school year. Will Haley spend it living it up in the present? Or will she put all her energy into ensuring her future?

FINAL WARNING

You have to trust the source before you heed the warning.

Hillsdale was down to the last few weeks of school, and the kids were getting testy. A blast of truly hot summertime weather had arrived just as the school's air-conditioning system went on the fritz, though miraculously, Principal Crum's enormous office still seemed like an icebox. Students were getting more disobedient and restless by the minute as the heat wave went to their heads. Irene, Shaun, Devon and Haley were no exception.

On the first day of finals, Shaun came barreling down the hallway dressed in combat boots and cutoff camouflage shorts, yelling at the top of his lungs and peeling off his shirt in protest of the heat. "We cannot solve for x in an oven. Are you mad, people? Spock? Spartacus? Beam me up to your frosty Bel-Air planet, Kirk Douglas, oh, please."

Haley thought Shaun might be suffering from heatstroke. She certainly felt as if she were. Worst of all, she couldn't even go home and bask in cooler air since her parents refused to turn on their brand-new central AC. "It's bad for the environment," Joan kept reminding her. Haley knew she was right, but it was nevertheless painful to sleep in the warm, sticky air that clung to the walls in her bedroom.

The heat wasn't the only thing Haley had to worry about. Principal Crum had just announced he was rejiggering the weighting scale on finals, so that they would count for much more of each student's final grade. It was an attempt to get the student body to collectively hit the books after an unusually bad year of standardized test results.

Principal Crum had also sent out individual warnings to students who were expected to get at least one D on their report cards, letting them know this was actually a golden opportunity to bring their grades up for the year.

"I can't believe he's only telling us this now,"

Haley said, fanning herself with a comic book in the lunchroom. "How was I supposed to know my grades had slipped that far? And he's giving us what, like, a few days to cram and pull them up?"

"Whatever," said Irene. "I think it's just another one of Crum's idle threats. He's done this before. My grades always come out pretty average in the end."

"He's just trying to scare everyone, perpetuate the cycle of fear," said Devon. "He does the same thing with that stupid colored alert system."

"Careful," Haley warned in a mock-serious tone. "We're currently on chartreuse."

"Don't you cats know that our school's academic ranking helps dictate what sort of development money they get for next year?" said Shaun. "I think Prince Crum is just a tin soldier too. But I think we should brace ourselves for the fact that this just might be the big one."

The four of them looked at each other intently. "Nah!" they all said.

"I've got to get to class," Haley said, getting up. "I've skipped Spanish so many times Ms. Frick could fail me for that alone."

"Traitor," Devon said, only half kidding.

"Deadbeat," Haley retorted.

As she was leaving the cafeteria, she bumped into Richie Huber, the perpetual senior who was always preying on younger girls. Coco De Clerq, Haley believed, had coined the term *vulture* to describe Richie and guys like him, who assumed underclassmen were easy. It was the first sign of life Haley had ever witnessed on planet De Clerq.

"Hey, come here for a sec," Richie said, motioning for Haley to step out into the hall and into his "office." "I've been wanting to ask you something," he said, and brushed the hair out of her eyes.

Ugh, you have got to be kidding me, Haley thought, totally grossed out by Richie's come-ons. *I only wish I could film this. Doesn't he realize how ridiculous he is?*

"How would you like to go to the prom with yours truly?" He put a finger to her lips. "Shhh, I know, sugar. You can't believe your luck. But just wait until prom night, baby. You won't believe how lucky you can get."

● ● ●

It appears Richie Huber has been stuck in high school for a lot longer than he claims, as those pickup tactics were clearly straight out of the seventies.

If you think it would be fun to toy with Richie, go to PROM on page 227. If you're too worried about Haley's grades to play around with anything or anyone, turn to CRAM FOR FINALS on page 223. Finally, if you think there are much, much, much more important things in life than report cards and finals, BLOW OFF

HOMEWORK and keep Haley hanging out with the originals Shaun, Irene and Devon on page 238.

People always say prom night is a night you'll never forget. If Richie takes Haley as his date, he may end up wishing he could erase all traces of the night from memory.

You can't force two people
together when they clearly
want to be kept apart.

The whole school had heard about Sasha and
Johnny's blowout fight on the night of the Battle of
the Bands. Johnny had waited until after he and
Sasha were alone together to lash into her about her
"lousy, distracted" performance and how it had cost
the Hedon their win. Lots of unforgivable things
were said that night. Photos were torn apart. Tears
were spilled. Sasha threw a ring Johnny had given to
her into a creek near his house. It looked as if the sun

over Hillsdale High's golden couple was finally about to set.

And most upset of all by that news were Cecily, Drew and Reese. At least, that was how it seemed to Haley.

Having witnessed the pair madly in love in Paris over spring break, Haley's friends just couldn't believe that Sasha and Johnny's relationship had been severed over something they both cared so deeply about: the band. It was unthinkable. Or rather, such a breakup *would* have been unthinkable just a few weeks prior.

The group sulked into Hap's Diner to collect on a free meal won during field day, though no one seemed to have much of an appetite. They picked at their french fries. They talked about—what else— Sasha and Johnny. Haley pointed out that the only time Sasha and Johnny had seemed to be spending together lately was at those "stupid" band practices. Cecily spoke up and said Sasha had recently confided that Johnny hadn't taken her on a real date in weeks. Then Reese added that Johnny had been complaining to the guys that Sasha seemed to care more about track practice than him, while Drew revealed that the pair voted Class Couple in the sophomore yearbook polls had stopped making out shortly after their trip to Paris.

"We just have to remind them why they got

together in the first place," Haley said, taking a half-hearted sip of her soda.

"And we have to get them to stop thinking about the band," added Cecily.

"And?" Drew added. "Aren't you forgetting something? We have to get Sasha to quit the track team."

"Wait a second," Reese began, though he quickly stopped once he saw the look on Drew's face, which said, *Come on, brother. We men stick together.*

"Why should Sasha have to quit track?" Haley demanded.

"I was wondering the same thing myself," said Cecily, folding her arms across her chest and glaring at Drew. "She can do both if she wants to. I don't see you quitting track so your lazy butt can focus on those silly video games of yours. And you take that garbage way more seriously than Johnny has ever taken the Hedon."

"What about you?" Haley asked, looking at Reese. "You're being awfully quiet. What do you think?"

"I, um . . . ," Reese said, hesitating and looking back and forth from Haley to Drew. "Well, I do think Sasha could have been a little better about managing her time. I guess."

"Oh no, he did not just say that," said Cecily, standing up and grabbing Haley's hand, dragging her out of Hap's and leaving Reese and Drew behind with the now-cold burgers and fries.

● ● ●

The classic divide of boys vs. girls, cats vs. dogs, strikes again.

So what's Haley going to do about it? If you feel strongly that Haley should forget Sasha and Johnny's differences and stay focused on the positive, REUNITE SASHA AND JOHNNY on page 233. If you think Haley and Cecily should turn their little debate into a battle of the sexes, go to BOYS VS. GIRLS on the next page.

Remember what your mother says: don't talk behind people's backs.

Rarely do problems
get solved
by open warfare.

Haley couldn't believe Reese had sided with Johnny. Or that he thought it was too much for Sasha to run track *and* play in the band. Did that mean Reese expected Haley to give up filmmaking, or athletics, or both, so she could focus all her time and attention on him? Was there only room in a girl's life for one passion?

The more she thought about it, the more upset she got. "Some nerve," Haley fumed later on the phone to Cecily. "Can you believe how backward those guys are?"

"Tell me about it," Cecily agreed. "Drew's the worst of all. I just heard he's been pushing Johnny to kick Sasha out of the band all along! He told Johnny he thought a *chick* would bring the Hedon *down*."

"I bet next he'll be telling you that track is too much of a guy's sport, and that you should stick to cheerleading," Haley said, egging her friend on.

"I told that boy he better not be meddling in other people's affairs."

By the time Haley and Cecily patched Sasha into their call, they weren't just mad, they were demanding blood. Boy blood. The following day at school, Sasha confronted Johnny at his locker and dumped a box of his things on the floor in front of him. Things that were all smashed to bits. Then she marched over to Zoe Jones, and in full view of Johnny, asked if there was room for a fifth band member in Rubber Dynamite. *Ouch.*

Cecily went one further. She photocopied a recent picture of Drew with his tattered old baby blanket, which he *still* slept with. She then papered it all over school, including the guys' locker room. He couldn't walk down a hall for the next year without someone making baby noises at him.

And finally, Haley broke up with Reese in the main courtyard, practically in front of the whole school, telling anyone who would listen he was a terrible kisser and, worse, a *prude*. After all that drama, the three girls spent the summer miserable, missing the boys and wondering just how things had ever gotten so out of hand.

Hang your head and go back to page 1.

Wet and wild can be a very potent combo.

On the evening of Senior SIGMA, more kids than Haley could count were piled in Richie Huber's swimming pool, sloshing water over the sides and into the yard. The Hubers' well-manicured lawn and patio were decorated to look like a Hawaiian beach luau, complete with a bonfire and meats roasting on a spit. Girls sipped frozen drinks under umbrellas while Richie and his boys tended to the skewers of shrimp, pork and beef. There was a reason for Haley to be there, but she couldn't help being tempted away from her objective by the delicious scent of Hawaiian barbecue wafting her way.

"Do you like this 'kini?" Whitney asked, lifting up her white tunic as she and Haley walked into the party, accompanied by a shell-shocked-looking Coco De Clerq. Coco had only just begun eating and speaking after several days of an all-out crisis following her horrific meltdown on the tennis court during the regionals. A loud and rowdy party was the last place on earth she should probably have been, but Coco had insisted. Haley had at least been able to convince her friend to sip some lukewarm consommé before they left the De Clerq mansion.

"Whitney, don't you think we have more important things to attend to than our outfits?" Haley said, pointing to Coco, who, in spite of the eighty-degree-plus temperature, was shivering. "Hang in there, kiddo. We'll find Ali," Haley added, squeezing Coco's hand.

As they stepped onto the pool deck, Haley felt a tap on her shoulder. She turned around, hoping to find Ali standing next to her, but instead it was Annie Armstrong. "Aloha," Annie said just as Dave Metzger appeared with a beer in his hand. Dave had a five o'clock shadow that looked like the beginnings of a goatee. *I never thought I'd see the day,* thought Haley. *Dave Metzger, the bearded beer drinker. Guess that's one thing he's not allergic to.*

"Um, Haley," Annie began tentatively. "Just the

person I wanted to see. Have you by chance heard anything about our teachers changing the weighting system on our grades for the year?"

"Not now," Haley said, annoyed to be bothered by the girl who had single-handedly sabotaged Hillsdale High's yearbook. Thanks to Annie, there likely wasn't going to be a *Talon* this year. Haley was shocked that Annie had the guts to show her face at a party for seniors, who were understandably pissed that they weren't going to have a bound memento of their last year of high school.

"Hey, nice skirt," Whitney broke in, admiring Annie's white ruffled mini.

"Actually I got this *falda* in *España*," Annie said, twirling around to show it off before taking a sip of Dave's beer.

"Look at that stitching—it's *gorgeous*!" Whitney exclaimed. "I should totally rip that off for my new line."

"Oh, I heard about your trunk show," Annie said. "Would you mind if I stopped by?"

"Not if you plan on spending some money." Whitney giggled. "Hi, by the way. I'm not sure we've ever met. I'm Whitney, Whitney Klein."

"Yeah, um, I know," said Annie, with a mixture of annoyance, embarrassment and pity. "I'm Annie Armstrong. We've gone to school together for, like, eight years."

"Oh, my gosh! Headstrong!" Whitney exclaimed.

"I totally didn't recognize you! Imagine that! I didn't know you partied."

Neither did I, thought Haley. "Listen, we're trying to find Coco's sister," she said impatiently, turning to address Dave. "Have you seen her? Or Spencer Eton, for that matter?"

"Up there," he said, not very helpfully pointing toward the most out-of-control part of the party.

At that moment, Richie called out, "Come and get it!" from the grill, which of course caused pandemonium. Kids came running from all directions, climbing out of the pool and trickling out of the poker game that had been going on inside.

"Hey, baby," Richie said, stepping out of their way and wrapping his arms around three more-than-willing freshmen. "Or should I say 'babies'?"

Vulture, Haley thought, using Coco's word for older guys who preyed on underclassmen because they assumed young girls were easy. Actually, Haley realized, freshman girls who showed up at senior parties usually were easy. Richie already had his tongue down one of the girls' throats.

"Hey, isn't that . . . Coco De Clerq?" a senior football player asked his buddy, nudging him toward Haley's trio. "Damn, what happened there? She looks like she could use a good bath."

"Shut up, you lout," Haley said, defending Coco while still scanning the crowd for Ali and Spencer. "She's had a rough . . . month."

208

"Sounds like she needs a drink," the lout said, and before Haley could stop him, he threw Coco, still clad in her tennis gear from two days prior, into the pool.

Haley and Whitney helped a drenched Coco up over the coping. Once she was safe, Haley said, "Hold on," and walked over to pants one of the fat-head seniors.

"What'sa matter, honey? You want some of this?" the jerk added, turning around so that everyone could get a full view of his manhood. "Hey, Coco, come back over here."

Haley was about to give up on this escapade and take Coco home when finally she spotted Spencer over near the house. She led the poor, wet, bedraggled Coco in his direction, noticing that strangely enough, even with a Jacuzzi full of girls next to him, Spencer didn't seem all that interested in getting either wet or wild. The same could not be said for Matt Graham, however, who was making out with one senior girl in the hot tub while groping another.

"I'm sorry," Coco blurted out as they confronted Spencer and Ali appeared by his side. Tears began rolling down Coco's cheeks. "I really mean it this time," she said between sobs. "I was hateful and jealous and terrible to you both. And I wouldn't be surprised if neither of you ever talked to me again. I just came to say . . . I really hope . . . you two are happy together. Because I . . . I . . . I . . . I love you both very much."

Ali and Spencer looked at each other, stunned, and not unaffected by the speech. Coco's mission accomplished, she turned to Haley and said, still sniffling, "Can you please take me home?"

● ● ●

Richie's house has always been an animal house, but that was a downright zoo. Guess there ain't no party like a seniors-just-before-graduation party, no?

So what do you think? Was Coco's apology authentic? And will Ali and Spencer finally forgive her? Here's a question: which De Clerq sister do you think Spencer *really* wants to be with?

To send Haley to see Whitney's new clothing designs unveiled, along with the De Clerq girls, go to WHITNEY'S TRUNK SHOW on page 187. Alternatively, find out why Annie is suddenly so worried about her grades on page 219, in ANNIE COMES TO HER SENSES.

If Haley thought Coco had already hit rock bottom, boy, was she mistaken. That little scene will go down in Hillsdale High history.

EDIT HOME MOVIES WITH DAD

Unfortunately, embarrassing moments are the ones you never forget.

Haley watched as her dad set up his laptop. Perry had spent weeks compiling the entire Miller family home movie collection, transferring it to digital, and uploading the files. Tonight, Perry planned to edit the footage into what he called "the perfect montage."

Haley had volunteered to help, mostly to have a say in which clips from her childhood made the final cut of a film she knew would be shown over, and over, and over again, to everyone from neighbors, to family members, to friends, to even the random postal worker or housekeeper.

"Dad, no way," Haley said, objecting to the very first clip he played on the screen. It was footage of an infant Haley spitting up on herself. He cut that in favor of peacefully sleeping baby Haley. She was holding her blanket and sucking her thumb. Next up was Haley at age two, perched in her high chair, sucking on a lemon, squinting and pursing her lips while drooling all over herself. "Not that, either," Haley commanded.

"Come on," Perry whined. "I call this one 'Sweet Tart.' Besides, you only get a few vetoes, so use them wisely."

"Fine," Haley sighed, giving in. To be honest, she was much more concerned about editing out footage from her brace-face and early training-bra periods.

"Awww, wook at dis one," Perry cooed a few minutes later.

Haley looked and was completely freaked out by the old footage of her mom breast-feeding Mitchell.

"Dad, that's gross," said Haley. "Next!"

"Wow, what a beautiful little girl you were," Perry said, deeply charmed by the ten-year-old Haley marching around the stage in a school play.

Haley felt a vibration at her hip. *Two text messages,* she realized. The first was from Whitney Klein: "Haley, in case you didn't get the invite, I'd LOVE IT if you could stop by my trunk show this week. I can't w8 for you to c my new collection!" Haley thought it was pretty cool that Whitney was now designing her own clothes, and she was glad the girl had finally found something to keep her from shoplifting her way across Bergen County.

Then Haley read the second text. *It's from Reese!* she thought, more than a little excited to read on. "Hey, Haley, we're headed over to Hap's later. Can you meet us? I have all those gift certificates from field day to use, and Sasha and Johnny just bailed. They're fighting. Again. Anyway, let's cash these in. Reese."

Haley looked up. *Maybe I should go,* she thought, wondering what it would do to her dad if she skipped out on their home movies date to go on a real date with Reese.

But Perry knew his daughter well enough to recognize a distracted look when he saw one. "So what did Reese have to say?" he asked, revealing that he knew a text had come from the cute boy next door without Haley having to say a word. "I get the feeling I may be editing home movies by myself for the rest of the evening. Don't worry about it, sweetie. You should go," said Perry with a smile. "Do you need me to give you a ride somewhere?"

● ● ●

Awwww, talk about sweet. How great is Haley's dad? He can be the coolest sometimes. And then other

times . . . not so much. Why, for instance, does he go so gaga over Haley's Dorkiest Home Videos?

If you think Reese's invitation to join him at Hap's is a no-brainer, go to page 198, FREE MEAL AT HAP'S. Or alternatively would you rather lend Whitney support at her first big TRUNK SHOW on page 187?

Two very different paths await Haley. Which one will produce further embarrassing moments? And which will make her wish she'd just stayed home with Dad?

BABYSIT WITH DEVON

Has anyone ever really sat on a baby?

"This giraffe. Has. A sticky tongue," Mitchell announced as a tall giraffe stretched its neck over the fence of the African animals exhibit and licked his hand.

"Ick," Devon's little sister, Shana, gasped. She was so tiny and delicate to begin with, next to the towering giraffe, she looked like a doll.

"Who wants ice cream?" Devon asked as a push-cart ice cream vendor approached.

"Affirmative," said Mitchell, while Devon's sister

just nodded, her already-saucerlike eyes growing even larger. Haley knew Devon wasn't exactly well-off. Okay, his family was downright poor. That he was spending his own hard-earned money from his job at Jack's Vintage Clothing to take the kids to the zoo only made her like him that much more. She thought it was pretty sweet the way he watched out for both of the kids and simultaneously paid attention to her.

"Here you go," Devon said, handing Haley an ice cream sandwich.

"Thanks," said Haley, not feeling at all as if she were missing out on anything by not being at the Battle of the Bands.

"We. Would like. To ride the. Carousel," said Mitchell, taking Shana's hand. Devon gave the kids a few coins each.

"They certainly seem to be getting along," said Haley.

"Yeah," Devon agreed. "We won't have to muzzle them." Haley laughed. She loved how easy and relaxed he was at this moment. She only wished she always brought out that side of Devon. "I'm really glad we came," he said.

"Oh?"

"Yeah, Shana doesn't get to play with other kids that often. We don't exactly live in the friendliest of neighborhoods," he added, referring to their railroad house in the worst part of the Floods.

"It won't always be that way," Haley said, trying to sound positive. "You'll finish high school, go to college—"

"Live out the American dream?" Devon interrupted. "Somehow, I don't think that's what's in store for me."

"Why not?"

"I don't know. I worked my butt off to get into that art school in New York, and what happened? They lost funding, and I ended up back where? In a stinking New Jersey public school with a lousy art program."

"Yeah," said Haley, "full of lousy kids like *me*."

"Sorry. It just seems like every time I get my hopes up and start thinking that things might actually change, I get smacked right back down into my place. The dirt-poor grunger from the wrong side of the tracks, literally. I feel like I shouldn't even bother trying anymore. Besides, it's not like anyone's really going to care when I bring home a lousy report card."

Haley tried to imagine what life must be like for Devon, having to work a steady job *and* constantly look after his kid sister. Who would have time for basic schoolwork? Much less for pursuing an art career.

While Devon collected the kids from the carousel, Haley felt her cell phone vibrate and checked to see whom the text message was from. It was, not surprisingly, Reese Highland. Gorgeous, easy, uncomplicated Reese, who seemed to get more interested in Haley the more time she spent with Devon. "Hey, Red, we'll miss you at Battle of the Bands tonight. Wish you could be there. But . . . a bunch of us are going to Hap's next week, to use those gift certificates we won at field day. Wanna join us?"

Devon looked at her from the carousel and smiled, his face much brighter than it had been only a few minutes before. It was a sight Haley wished she could see more of—like, all the time.

● ● ●

Devon's address certainly isn't Easy Street, that's for sure. But everyone has some kind of obstacle to overcome, don't they? It's just that right now Haley's biggest problem—deciding which boy to date—sounds a whole lot more superficial than Devon's ongoing family, financial and artistic dilemmas.

If you want to keep Haley and Devon together despite their differences, turn to FINAL WARNING on page 193. To send Haley for that FREE MEAL AT HAP'S with Reese, turn to page 198.

In a hard-knock life, doors are rarely opened for you. You have to kick them in yourself.

ANNIE COMES TO HER SENSES

It's never too late for a rude awakening.

By midafternoon on the last Wednesday before finals, Haley had begun to notice a theme developing in all her classes. Every one of her teachers so far that day had lectured them on how the school's test scores were at a record low. They claimed the students of Hillsdale High had been slacking off that spring and that the school's academic performance was in an awful slump because of it.

Just as Coach Tygert began a similar speech while addressing his honors history class, however halfheartedly, Principal Crum's voice came crackling over the loudspeaker. "Attention, students of Hillsdale," he began. "Hillsdale High has never ranked this low on the state's roster of public schools, not in the history of our district," he said. "Of course, the school has only been open for nine years. But I do not want to set an unfortunate precedent!" He cleared his throat with a phlegmy cough. "We need our test scores to rise dramatically in order to finish out the year with respectable numbers. Therefore, the grading structure has been changed for your finals. As of today, your final exams will count for fifty percent of your grade."

Boos echoed throughout the hallways.

"Fifty percent," Annie said, horrified and turning sheet white. "Great Scott, the rumors were true."

"Thank you, students. That is all!" Crum finished sternly. And with that, he signed off.

"Quiet down, please," Mr. Tygert said calmly.

"Mr. Tygert, is it true that the teachers all got together to change the grading system in order to increase their salaries?" Dave asked from the back of the room.

"Actually, Dave, that's not quite true, but you are on to something. I will tell you that the school's overall ranking does affect its budget for the year, and in a very small way, our salaries," he admitted. "But making sure you students get the best education possible is certainly our primary focus. We don't want the quality of education at Hillsdale to decline. And we always want you kids to do your best."

Annie's formerly relaxed expression had completely tensed up. "I don't know what I was thinking," she mumbled guiltily. "How will I ever get through seven finals? My GPA! My precious GPA! We have to get our study group back together this weekend and cram like crazy. It's our only hope."

Dave nodded solemnly in agreement.

At that moment, a text message appeared on Haley's cell phone from Ali De Clerq, warning her that the glad-hander forever hovering somewhere in the senior class, Richie Huber, was planning to ask her to prom. He thought, as all upperclassman guys did, that because she was a sophomore, she would be an "easy" date. Whatever that meant.

Before Haley could even contemplate what her answer to Richie would be, Annie Armstrong was handing her a detailed list of possible times their study group could get together over the next few days.

"Wait, how is this already typed?" Haley asked, realizing that the old Annie had most definitely returned.

● ● ●

Welcome back, Annie! Now get your pen. Apparently it took the school experiencing a catastrophic academic slump to snap her out of her slacker stupor. Should Haley be worried about her own GPA?

If you think Haley will take Principal Crum's warning very seriously, have her try to improve her GPA and CRAM FOR FINALS on page 223. If you think it's all just a bunch of smoke and mirrors, a scare tactic to force students into extra studying to ratchet up the school's academic standing, you can either (a) have Haley BLOW OFF HOMEWORK on page 238 with the ultimate artistic types, Shaun, Devon and Irene, or (b) send her to the PROM with the octopus-handed upperclassman Richie Huber on page 227. Haley's just lucky she won't be the only sophomore there.

CRAM FOR FINALS

If copying someone else's work outside a testing zone with their permission isn't cheating, it's certainly a gray area.

The Saturday before final exams, Haley and Hannah arrived at the Armstrong residence to study. Make that to do the best studying of their life. The girls came prepared, armed with schoolbooks, charts and pie graphs, laptop computers, an overhead projector and stern focus. Since it had been announced that their final exams were going to count for fifty percent of their grades, the pressure was on, in the most extreme sense.

"Hi," Annie greeted them with an all-business

demeanor as she welcomed the study group members into her house. She was no longer wearing one of her loose, flowing sundresses from Spain, which she'd been living in lately. Tonight, she had on her old reading glasses, a white button-down shirt tucked into a skinny pair of knee-length khaki shorts, and her best loafers. Haley admired her outfit, including the braided belt that matched the barely visible tassel on her shoes, remembering why her friend had a reputation for being type A.

"I figure if we cover one week of Ms. Frick's outline every fifteen minutes, we'll get through Spanish in a single night," Annie said as they walked swiftly toward the kitchen, where Mrs. Armstrong had laid out a brain-building feast: lots of leafy greens, whole grains and protein.

Even though Annie looked calm, Haley could tell from her tone just how nervous she was about finals. Clearly, she was now regretting her half-semester siesta, but Haley guessed Annie would come to look back on that time in her life very fondly. After all, with those Armstrong genes, she was unlikely to take such a long break ever again in her life.

Before Haley had a chance to finish the celery and peanut butter she was munching on, Sebastian walked in. Haley was *shocked*. She'd barely seen him in weeks, and hadn't spoken to him once after she'd caught him with his supermodel ex-girlfriend, Mia Delgado, who had come to town from Spain to stay with the Shopes at the tail end of spring break. Sebastian looked guiltily in Haley's direction.

"I figured it would be easier to all study from the same notes," Hannah said, handing them each a packet. "Hope you don't mind, but I figured mine were best. They usually are," Hannah added, without a hint of arrogance.

"Thank you!" Annie said genuinely, realizing that Hannah had probably just saved her whole academic career, even though, with Annie out of the way, Hannah would have had the number-one slot in the class locked down. "I don't know what to say. You're . . . my hero."

"Don't thank me," Hannah said, as if she were unworthy of thanks. "Thank my voice recognition program."

"Voice recognition program?" Dave echoed.

"Well," Hannah announced, turning on her computer, "I wouldn't have such accurate notes without this device here. I built it last summer. I can record all the lectures in class with this dictaphone function. It then transcribes all of them for me, editing out any repetitive passages and organizing thoughts into a coherent structure."

These are the most organized, meticulous notes I've ever seen, Haley thought as she flipped through the pages.

"Robot notes?" Dave asked with a giggle. "Why didn't I think of that?"

After a few hours of going through each page of the packet aloud, everyone miraculously seemed to have a handle on the material. In fact, when Hannah quizzed them all rigorously at the end of the session, no one missed a single question.

As everyone but Annie stumbled out the door at almost two a.m., Sebastian pulled Haley aside. "I want . . . There are so many things to say to you," he said. His warm peanut butter breath sent a shiver through her. "May I take you to dinner? After finals, of course. It's *muy importante.*"

Haley was skeptical. At this point, she just wanted to get through exam week without any further distractions. Sebastian had long ago missed his shot with her. Or had he?

● ● ●

What do you think? Do you still trust Sebastian? Should Haley hear him out? Or does that dog deserve to be left in the yard?

If you want Haley to concentrate on getting through finals before deciding what to do with the next three months of her life, turn to SUMMER SCHEDULING on page 252. To accept Sebastian's dinner invitation, turn to DATE WITH SEBASTIAN on page 248. If Haley does go, she's sure to find out what's on the tip of his tongue.

**Occasionally, prom does live
up to its promise of being
the party of the year.**

There were good things and bad things about going to the prom with Richie "Octopus Arms" Huber. On the negative side, he tried to feel Haley up two minutes after picking her up. On the positive side, once they'd arrived at the massive hotel ballroom where the dance was being held, Richie was so distracted by all the other ladies in the room, he left Haley alone. At least for a little while.

"Wow! You look *awesome*! I so knew peach would be your color," Whitney gasped as Haley walked up in a Whitney Klein original. Though Haley had been skeptical about whether a pastel would work with her auburn hair and creamy complexion, Whitney had been right. The peach strapless number was pretty luscious on her.

Whitney, meanwhile, was in a layered yellow chiffon minidress that made her look like a cupcake—in the best possible way. "I love the yellow on you," Haley said, adding, "How come I didn't see that dress on your rack?"

"It was a last-minute experiment," said Whitney. "I think I came up with a new stitch." She held up the hem of her dress, revealing just a bit too much of whatever was underneath.

Haley shoved Whitney's hem down. "Show me later. So where's Coco?"

"Oh. Yeah. She's in the bathroom on another one of her crying jags. Her date, Allen, told her she looked nice, and it just . . . set her off. You know how she's been lately."

It was true. Ever since Coco had finally gotten in touch with her feelings, it was as if the floodgates had opened. Everything that had been buried since the beginning of Coco's adolescence was now bubbling up to the surface. She cried when she saw babies or puppies. Movie trailers made her puddle. Seeing Spencer and Ali together? That filled her with so much simultaneous love, remorse and regret that she sometimes practically hyperventilated.

"Maybe we should go check on her," said Haley.

"Who's ready for a drink?" Richie said, his right eyebrow raised as if to say, *And you know what kind of drink I'm talking about.* He was holding three cups of punch, which he set down on a table. Then he took out his silver monogrammed flask.

"Whitney?" Richie asked, holding up a cup of the spiked punch.

"No thanks. Ever since my mom entered AA and I saw what it's done for her, I've been totally against drinking."

"But your mom was never an alcoholic," Haley countered.

Whitney just shrugged. "I think it's a good philosophy."

"What about you, Haley?" Richie said, offering the cup to her.

Haley looked around the room. She hardly knew any of the seniors and juniors present—at least, not well enough to talk to them. But they did seem to be having a good time. The prom theme, "Her Hillsdale Highness," totally worked, what with all the gilded mirrors and brocade curtains in the ballroom, and the two thrones that had been placed on the stage. Haley then looked at her date. Richie, when he wasn't manhandling her or six other girls at once, could be sort of fun. The question was, would he be fun or dangerous after they'd both had something to drink?

If you want to accept Richie's offer, turn to page 259. Otherwise, keep reading.

• • •

"No thanks, Richie," Haley replied. "Maybe later. Right now, we've got to go check on Coco." She took Whitney by the hand and dragged her off toward the bathroom.

They found Coco sitting in the ladies' room on a settee and clutching a dinner napkin, which she was using to dab her damp eyes, listening to the bathroom attendant tell her saga about her illegal emigration from Mexico. Despite the tears and the forlorn look on her face, Coco looked beautiful. Whitney had decided to put her in purple taffeta, which was just the right shade to draw some flecks of color out of her eyes. The dress had a tight corset bodice and a full skirt that poufed out over the edge of the settee like the petals of a flower. "I'm going to put you in touch with Jorge, our groundskeeper," Coco said, sniffling. "He has a fabulous immigration lawyer. I'm sure he can help"—Coco's voice caught—"bring your little boy up from Oaxaca."

"Thank you, miss," the woman said. "You are an angel."

If she only knew, Haley thought. "Why so sad?" she asked, kneeling down next to Coco. "Don't you know there's a whole party out there waiting for you? The Coco I know loves parties."

"Um, I think that was the Coco you used to know," said Whitney. Haley's eyes widened and she glared at Whitney over her shoulder as if to say, *You're not helping matters!*

"I—I—I . . . ca-can't," Coco started, "believe . . . our immigration policy is so cruel."

"Come on," Haley said, holding out her hand. Coco tentatively reached out, and Haley pulled her to her feet. "Ladies, I think we have some dancing to do."

The trio took the dance floor by storm, carving out a space for themselves right in front of the band. Soon, practically every guy in the room was trying to hit on them, but they were having none of it. Once the senior girls saw that the sophomores weren't after their dates, they joined the dance party too, and then things really picked up. Haley was having a blast. So, clearly, was Whitney. And for the first time in weeks, Coco was genuinely *smiling*.

The prom king and queen were eventually announced. Ali De Clerq and Coco's date, one of the senior football players, ascended to the stage to accept the honors and were then coupled off for the king and queen's official dance.

"Thought you might need a dance partner for this one," Spencer said, suddenly appearing at Coco's side. He then added, "That is, if Haley and Whitney will allow me to cut in."

"She's all yours," said Whitney.

Spencer Eton and Coco De Clerq began swaying to the slow song. Ali looked over at them from across the dance floor, smiled and gave a big thumbs-up. All in all, it was turning out to be a great night, even if the boy Haley wished to be dancing with wasn't even in the room. And even if her date was constantly trying to stick a hand down her dress.

● ● ●

That was a steamy slow dance for Coco and Spencer. Clearly, the prom brought out the warm feelings they've been harboring.

Have Haley join Coco to watch Ali De Clerq, the newly crowned prom queen, graduate from Hillsdale High at ALI'S GRADUATION on page 256. If you think Haley's work here is done and want her to reconnect with Reese, Cecily and Sasha, send her to LAST DAY OF SCHOOL on page 242.

No matter how many tears were shed by Coco, that turned out to be one legendary prom night. Now Haley just needs to find someone to dance with.

REUNITE SASHA
AND JOHNNY

**True love can never be denied,
at least not permanently.**

"**N**ice!" said Cecily, holding up the T-shirt she and
Haley had cocreated at the kiosk at the mall.

A picture of Sasha and Johnny standing in front
of the Eiffel tower in berets and black and white
striped shirts was silk-screened onto a white tank
top for Sasha.

"It's perfect," Cecily said, smiling at the job well
done.

"So is this one," said Haley. She held up the large
counterpart they'd made for Johnny. Flipping the

shirt over, Haley revealed the words BEST COUPLE printed in block letters across the back. "I'll have Sasha come to my house in twenty minutes."

"And I'll tell Drew to make sure Johnny shows up at Reese's in about an hour," said Cecily, texting her boyfriend.

Haley took a moment to check her own messages and found that there were two: one from Coco, inviting Haley to her older sister's graduation celebration, and another from Annie Armstrong, who had just narrowly escaped a disastrous hit to her GPA. Annie was getting a group together to go away to an academic summer camp and wanted to know if Haley might join them.

When Sasha rang the doorbell later, Mr. Miller answered with a wide smile. "How's my favorite classic rock fan?" he asked.

"I am a lonesome hobo," said Sasha. "I threw it all away. Talking bear mountain picnic massacre blues."

Mr. Miller raised an eyebrow, accepting Sasha's challenge. "You wanna ramble? Ye shall be changed. When the night comes falling from the sky. When the ship comes in."

"Thanks, Mr. M. I needed that."

"The girls are up in Haley's room," he said, returning to the pile of film reels strewn around the living room floor.

"Got it, chief," said Sasha, making her way upstairs.

Haley and Cecily's plan was to first let Sasha vent about her fight with Johnny. They figured that she would eventually open up, admitting to herself just how bad she felt about losing the Battle of the Bands.

Ten minutes later, the plan was working. Sasha was finally allowing herself to feel the full spectrum of emotions that she had been bottling up over the past week. "I really miss him," she said, choking back a sob.

"Here, close your eyes," Haley said. Sasha obliged, and they pulled the tank top on over her head. "Don't open them," Haley warned as they led her downstairs and outside to where Johnny and the boys were playing basketball in Reese's driveway. "Okay, now you can open them," Haley instructed.

Johnny let the ball roll into the grass.

"I'm so so sorry," Sasha said, rushing to him and collapsing in his arms.

Johnny couldn't resist that face, even if it was all puffy and teary-eyed. "It's okay," he said. "I was a complete jerk. And an idiot. And a fool. I was a jerk idiot fool."

"But I should have realized it was impossible to run track and be in the band. What was I thinking?"

"You were trying to stay true to who you are, and to also try something new and help out me and the band at the same time. Which I totally respect."

"I should've made a choice. But don't worry, I've

made one now. I can't give up track. Or soccer. I love them too much. So, I'm starting my solo career, as of now. I don't think it's healthy for us to always be talking about the band. This way I can go back to just being your girlfriend. I mean, if that's what you want."

"That's the only thing I want." They kissed and officially made up.

"Thank goodness," said Cecily. "I couldn't take listening to her sob on the phone one more time."

It was at that moment that Sasha and Johnny noticed each other's shirt. They each turned and saw the BEST COUPLE stamp on the back.

"You mean . . ."

"Yeah, doofus, you were elected Best Couple right before you broke up," said Cecily.

Sasha hugged her two best friends. "How psyched are we that we get to spend the summer together?" she said as Reese came up and put his slightly sweaty arms around Haley.

"I'm certainly not complaining," he said, kissing Haley on the cheek.

● ● ●

Well, kids, the Hillsdale High school year is winding down. To stick close to Reese, Sasha and Cecily for the summer, turn to LAST DAY OF SCHOOL on page 242. Alternatively, send Haley to brainiac camp with Annie

Armstrong in SUMMER SCHEDULING on page 252 or to see ALI'S GRADUATION on page 256.

Three months is a long time in a young life. Better make sure Haley is with the people she wants to spend the summer with now. Otherwise, she may not see them again until fall, her junior year.

BLOW OFF HOMEWORK

You only get one shot at final exams.

After school, Haley, Irene, Shaun and Devon walked by the library, which was completely packed with kids studying for finals. There wasn't an empty seat in the place.

"You so could not pay me to be in there," Irene said as they peered through the tinted library windows. "The AC is still out. They must be roasting alive."

"Fools. Crum actually tricked them into studying," vented Devon.

Shaun dashed over to the library door and threw it open, then yelled inside, "Copious amounts of knowledge can be bad for digestion." He farted, quite loudly, for effect. Fortunately, the on-duty librarian was away from her desk and missed the outburst. "Hey, I'm just warning you!" Shaun called out as someone threw a book at him. "Sheesh."

"So, what are we doing this afternoon?" asked Irene.

"I'm free as a bird. You?" said Devon.

"Welcome, you are," offered Shaun, "to dip your toes in my still waters."

"Yeah, let's go swimming," agreed Devon. "Haley, you wanna ditch and dip?"

"Well, I do have a final paper due in my English class that I was hoping to finish up this afternoon."

"Come on," said Devon. "You're sailing through that class."

"I've got a B-minus," said Haley. "My parents will not call that 'sailing.' "

"Grades don't mean anything, really," said Irene. "They're certainly not the most accurate measure of a person's wisdom, intelligence or worth. Why do you let them tell you who you are?"

"Uh, because in order to get into college, you need a certain GPA. You have your art, which means you don't need to worry about grades as much. But me? I seriously doubt one of my little home movies is going to get me into Brown." Her three friends looked at her with puppy-dog eyes. She wrestled with the invitation. *I certainly don't want to study on this sunny, muggy day. But finals are worth fifty percent of our grades. It would be totally irresponsible of me to go.*

"Fine, stay here, then," said Irene, who seemed personally offended by Haley's indecision. "We'll think of you with your nose stuck in the books while we're relaxed, cool in the pool." The trio began marching toward Devon's car.

Haley glanced into the library again. The kids inside looked trapped, like hamsters in a cage, spinning there on their little wheels. *So what if I don't get straight As for once?* she rationalized. *It's not going to kill me. I've been a model student my whole life. What's one year? Besides, everyone knows junior-year grades count the most with colleges.*

"Wait!" Haley called, walking swiftly to catch up. "Guys, I'm coming," she said. "Even though my parents are going to kill me, and I don't have a swimsuit."

"Sure you do, lady," said Shaun.

"Where?" Haley asked.

"Right here," Devon said, raising an eyebrow and pinching her arm lightly. "Your birthday suit."

● ● ●

Haley's GPA was looking pretty good. That is, until she dove into the deep end with the slackers. If you're curious to find out how these rebels do on their exams with-

out studying one lick, go to page 261, REPORT CARDS ARRIVE. If you think there's still time to salvage Haley's academic career, send her to a rigorous sleepaway camp in the Berkshires with the newly reformed Annie Armstrong on page 252, SUMMER SCHEDULING.

Now there's only one person left to blame if Haley flunks any of her classes. Yep, that would be you.

LAST DAY OF SCHOOL

**Summer smells like teen spirit.
And hot dogs, bug spray
and sunscreen.**

The last-period bell sounded on the last day of school, making it official: school was out for summer. Haley walked down the messy hallway with her empty book bag and a liberated skip in her step. She'd already cleaned out her locker and returned the last of her school library books, so her load was literally much lighter. As Haley looked around at the mayhem, her face said it best: *What a disaster zone!* The locker area was filled with students dumping mounds of loose papers, old notebooks and random trash. A team of janitors could barely remove the trash cans in time to make way for the next round of junk.

I sure hope they're recycling, Haley thought, making a mental note to put her mom on the case for next year. There was enough pulp here to provide paper for schoolkids in an African village for a year.

"Babe, you win the pack rat award," Sasha said to Johnny, who was dumping his third load of detritus into a can. From the looks of it, Johnny hadn't even made a dent in his locker yet.

"Disgusting, isn't it?" Johnny said with pride, pulling a rotten banana peel from under a stack of untouched textbooks. He seemed excited to have excavated the most disgusting item so far.

"Dude," said Drew, wrinkling his nose, "you're killing my environment."

In the distance, Haley noticed Ryan McNally busy cleaning out someone else's locker, with his container of biodegradable cleaning products and a clear blue recycling bag by his side. *Johnny could use the Cleanup Kid's services right about now,* Haley thought.

"I totally forgot you even had this sweatshirt," Cecily said to Drew, pulling a gray hoodie from the depths of his locker. "I haven't seen this since, like, October." Cecily, already done cleaning out her own ultratidy locker, had decided to help tackle her boyfriend's mess.

"Don't get any ideas," Sasha said jokingly to Johnny, realizing that the puppy-dog eyes he'd just given her meant he wanted girlfriend help too. "I'm not *touching* anything in there."

Johnny laughed, and shrugged as if it had been worth the attempt.

"Yo, Miller," Drew said, seeing Haley coming up behind them. Cecily was too busy chipping off a dried wad of purple gum stuck to the inside of Drew's locker to properly greet her.

"You're done already?" Sasha asked Haley. "Well, I guess you and Reese are both pretty neat." At that moment, Reese Highland appeared, shaking his head disapprovingly at his friends' wasted lockers.

Just then, Padma Monahar, a senior who was on the soccer team with Sasha and Haley, approached, her pretty, long black hair brushing her shoulders.

"I just wanted to say goodbye and good luck to you two," Padma said. "I would ask you to sign my yearbook, but we don't have them!"

"Hey, congrats," said Sasha. "Coach Tygert said you're going to try to play for Brown next year. That's great."

"Yeah, we'll see," Padma admitted modestly.

"Well, it certainly makes me feel better," Sasha said earnestly. "I can't tell you how sorry I am that I blew our last game of the season. You deserved a better finish at Hillsdale than that."

"Thanks, Sash," said Padma. "I'm just glad to see

you've got your focus back. You guys will have to come visit me in Providence, check out the college life."

"Sold," said Sasha. "We'll be up in the fall. Not on a game day, of course."

"Of course," Padma agreed. "See you tomorrow at graduation."

"Wouldn't miss it," said Haley, suddenly even more excited about becoming a junior next year. If that was possible.

The following day, Haley and Reese walked down the pathway behind the school toward the football field. Rows of white folding chairs had been set up along risers on the grass, along with a podium, microphones and speakers. Haley held Reese's hand. He had on the same navy suit and crisp white shirt he'd worn to the homecoming dance back in the fall, and looked every bit as handsome. Gradually, parents, teachers and fellow students started to fill the bleachers. Sasha and Johnny made their way toward them, along with Cecily and Drew.

Once they were all settled, music blasted over the loudspeaker, and before long, the senior class appeared in the distance, standing in two long lines. They began marching across the field two by two, cloaked in gold and blue satin gowns, wearing caps with tassels bearing the last two digits of their graduation year.

After the senior class was seated, Principal Crum

took the podium. A few boos escaped from the senior class—he had, after all, shut down the yearbook. But much to Haley's surprise, Principal Crum was eventually able to command everyone's attention with his high hopes for this class as they sailed off to meet their bright futures.

"BS," Johnny coughed, not buying Crum's parent-pleasing speech for one second.

"Move to Hollywood, Crum Bum," Drew joked. Still, Haley couldn't help being stirred by the moment. Soon enough, she and her friends would be up there.

"Look, there's Coco," Cecily said, spotting Coco sitting in the front row with Whitney, her parents and some other De Clerq relatives. "Looks like Grandma Starla made an appearance for Ali's graduation. Why does she always have lipstick on her teeth?"

"She's on husband number five at the moment," Sasha whispered. "Coco, welcome to your future."

"Can you believe Ali got into Yale?" whispered Cecily.

"Uh, hardly," said Sasha. "Guess the legacy pull is still stronger than we think."

"There may have been other . . . attractive qualities on her application," said Cecily. "I hear Yale will soon be building a new De Clerq dorm."

"Ah," said Sasha. "Makes sense. Ali couldn't be expected to live in old digs."

"Congratulations to this year's graduating class of Hillsdale High!" Principal Crum announced as he handed out the last of the diplomas, and the seniors simultaneously jumped to their feet, took off their caps and tossed them into the air. In that one frozen second, with all the gold and blue caps framed against the bluest of blue skies, Haley couldn't help wishing that those graduation caps would stay up in the air just a little longer, so that things would stay this perfect for as long as possible.

I can't wait to be a junior, but I'm definitely not ready to be a senior, Haley realized. She had finally settled in at Hillsdale High. She dreaded the thought of leaving another town, another school and another set of friends behind.

THE END

DATE WITH SEBASTIAN

Saying goodbye to a friend is never fun. Saying goodbye to an ex-boyfriend, possibly for the rest of your life, that's downright torture.

Haley waved to Mrs. Shope as she dropped Sebastian off in front of the Green Burrito, a Mexican restaurant in the center of town. Haley had only been standing there for five minutes, and she was dressed in the lightest possible summer sundress, but in the muggy heat, she was already starting to bead up.

"Haley, *hola!*" Sebastian said as he came over to

hug her. "I'm so sorry I'm late. I never like to keep a beautiful girl waiting."

"Yeah, I've noticed," said Haley, realizing they were already starting out on the wrong foot. "I'm ready for some air-conditioning," Haley said, wiping her forehead discreetly to make sure it wasn't glistening.

"It's *muy caliente* but you are looking even hotter. As always," he said, holding the door open for her.

Wow, was Sebastian always this cheesy? she wondered, seeing through and reading between his oh-so-bad pickup lines. A man wearing a sombrero greeted them and immediately escorted them to a cozy table in the back. Sebastian had reserved the most private space in the house. After they'd eaten a basket of warm tortilla chips with spicy salsa and ordered their entrées, Sebastian leaned in and took Haley's hand in his.

"Haley," he said. "I didn't want to tell you this while you were studying for finals." He paused dramatically. "I'm going home to Spain for the summer."

"Seriously?" Haley asked, not all that surprised. "Well, cool. When are you coming back?"

"That is the hard part," he said. "I am not really sure if I am coming back to Hillsdale, *mi amiga*."

Haley cringed at the familiar form of address she had also heard him use with Mia Delgado.

249

"I don't want to leave you," he said. Haley saw his dark brown eyes getting misty. "On this one hand, I miss my homeland so much, and my family."

"I'm sure there are other people you also miss," Haley said briskly.

"Yes, that's true," said Sebastian. "Friends. And the men who work our fields."

"And, perhaps, Mia Delgado?" Haley asked, dropping her bomb on him.

"Well, y-yes," Sebastian stuttered. "Mia is a friend. A friend I have had for a very long time."

Haley took a gulp of her ice water, trying to get rid of a lump in her throat. She had never been dropped for another girl before. And it wasn't fun.

"You, Haley," he said, and reached across the table to touch her hand again, ". . . are more than reason to stay. You are a beautiful *muchacha,* inside and out." He gazed romantically into her hazel eyes. "I cannot imagine not ever seeing you again." He paused. "But . . . Mia . . . she and I have this history, this deep, complicated *pasado.* Tell me, do you ever think it is possible to love two people at one time?"

"I think it's possible to convince yourself you love two people at once, and for that to make you act confused, selfish, inconsiderate and rude when the truth is, you love only yourself," said Haley, gathering up her things. "I think that's possible."

"Where are you going, *mi amor*?"

"Have a safe trip back to Spain, *amigo*. Mia can have you, for all I care."

As Sebastian watched her walk out of the restaurant, he realized he'd just made the biggest mistake of his life.

THE END

SUMMER SCHEDULING

Being a good student
brings its own rewards.

Thanks to Hannah Moss and her amazingly organized notes and study guides, Haley, Hannah, Annie,
Dave and Sebastian were the only students in Ms.
Frick's class to get perfect scores on the final exam.
Between the yearbook Haley had rescued from disaster and the way she was cleaning up on her grades, it
was turning out to be a banner year, even if she had
lost Sebastian Bodega to his former Spanish sweet-
heart. On the last day of school, as the class ranks

were being tabulated, Haley sat at a lunch table with Hannah and Annie awaiting the results.

"I'm not sweating it," Haley said as Dave arrived in the cafeteria, carrying a stack of sealed envelopes with their ranks inside.

"Not me. I can't stand the suspense," said Annie, bouncing around in her seat. She and Dave had much more at risk here, since they had sleepwalked through half of the semester. "Dave, the envelope, please!" Dave handed out the envelopes to the proper recipients, passing Haley hers last. Then he did a drumroll with his fingers on the lunch table.

"Okay," said Annie. "On the count of three, we all open at once."

"No matter what's in your envelope," Dave professed to Annie, "you'll always be my number one."

"One, two, three," Haley said speedily, tearing into her envelope before the last word had even left her mouth. As she tried to digest what her report said, she looked around to gauge her friends' reactions. Hannah looked as if she might faint, Annie looked as if she might cry, and Dave nodded as if he'd suspected all along exactly what he found inside. As tears streamed down Annie's face, Haley realized they were tears of relief, not disappointment. *Guess Annie's rank didn't slip that much after all,* Haley thought, and looked back down at her own piece of paper.

There are three hundred and ninety-two kids in our class. And I'm number . . . two? she realized gleefully. *That can't be.*

"So, what are you?" Annie asked.

"You first," said Haley.

"I'm still just number four," Annie gushed. "Thank goodness. And thanks to Hannah's brilliant notes. What are you?"

"I'm number one," Hannah said confidently, setting her paper down. "I have the highest rank in the class."

"What? Congratulations!" Haley exclaimed. "That's amazing! Though I can't say I'm surprised."

"Lucky number three," said Dave. Haley noticed that Annie winced a little at hearing this news. Dave had risen above her in the ranks. They all turned to look at Haley.

"Do I have to even say it out loud? Number two."

Annie looked shocked. Clearly, she had spent the year underestimating the new girl. Haley considered it good form that she didn't openly pout.

Within seconds, Sebastian Bodega sauntered over to the table and sat down.

"Are you guys ready to party or what?" he asked, doing a little dance in his seat. "School is over. Yah-yah!"

"Uh, we have to fill out our summer camp applications and get them in the mail today," explained Annie, pulling a stack of camp brochures out of her book bag. "We're already late as it is. And I think I've done enough partying for one semester."

"So you would send me back to *España* for good, without one last celebration?"

Haley's face went blank. She suddenly understood that Sebastian was seriously considering going back to Spain and not returning to Hillsdale for junior year. She didn't quite know how she felt about that. On the one hand, he deserved to be banished for inviting his ex-girlfriend to town without telling her. But she was also struck by a deep nostalgia for all the times they had spent together. She also wondered what camp and her junior year would be like if the old group wasn't all together. *Just when things were starting to feel settled,* thought Haley, sensing another big wave of changes.

THE END

ALI'S GRADUATION

Every end is also a beginning—according to valedictorians across the U.S.A.

Haley, Whitney and Coco sat in the folding chairs at the graduation ceremony, wondering how it would feel to be processing in a cap and gown in just a couple of years. For the first time in Haley's life, it all seemed real. High school had an end date. In the not-too-far-off future, she and her friends would be going to *college.*

Ali was headed to Yale in the fall, a surprisingly good school for a not-so-good girl. Apparently, Ali had a better head on her shoulders than Haley had first suspected. Haley wondered if there would be invitations to visit New Haven with Coco in the fall. There wasn't much time to get in good with the elder De Clerq. This summer, Ali would be touring Europe using the plane tickets and train passes her parents had bought for her for graduation.

On the other side of Coco was . . . Spencer Eton. And he was actually *holding Coco's hand*. Coco had given Ali and Spencer homemade DVDs that morning, which she and Haley had spent all weekend assembling. It had taken some serious digging and a little help from Perry Miller and his editing equipment, but Haley had managed to sift through the De Clerq home movie reels and videotapes and find some adorable little nuggets.

Ali had cried as she watched the footage of the two sisters playing in the bath together as babies, playing in the sand together as toddlers, playing in dance class together as little girls. Spencer wasn't as visibly moved by watching his tape, but Haley did catch him smiling and chuckling a few times as he witnessed a much earlier version of himself being fought over by two elementary-aged De Clerqs. Clearly, this was a long-standing family tradition.

Most importantly, the home movies had cemented Ali and Spencer's reconciliation with Coco. All was now right with the world. Ali and Coco were behaving like sisters again, with Spencer devoting equal time to each of them, though clearly his romantic

257

intentions had only ever been toward Coco. Even though Spencer and Ali had gotten very close over the past few months, they had never crossed the line beyond just being friends. Coco was and would always be the De Clerq he was infatuated with.

As Ali walked up to the podium and accepted her diploma, Spencer beamed at Coco. Haley gave it a week before they were officially dating. She figured having Ali away at school would probably change things between them, most likely for the better.

Even though Haley had no one to squeeze *her* hand at present, she felt good about the close of her first year at Hillsdale High and hopeful about the coming fall. Because of her, at least in part, Coco had gone from being the class bee-yotch to being a state-ranked tennis star who was actually kind of pleasant to hang out with. And Whitney, instead of being locked up for her shoplifting habit, was now a full-fledged fashion designer. Haley had just heard that two local boutiques would be carrying the WK dress line come fall. It was kind of miraculous to see how much one person could accomplish when she put her mind to something.

Besides, Haley knew her own time in the spotlight would soon come.

THE END

DRUNKEN DISASTER

Boys seem to grow tentacles when they drink.

At first, being tipsy at the prom with Richie Huber was a blast. They danced. He belted out numbers with the band. They even spent some time commanding the stage together, singing into the mike next to the lead singer.

But the more Richie's flask emptied into both of their cups, the more bold and obnoxious they became. Haley was soon plopping down at tables with juniors and seniors she'd never met before and introducing herself. Richie, meanwhile, was dancing up to his classmates, elbowing the guys out of the way, and grinding up against the girls. By eleven-thirty, Haley and Richie had earned themselves the title of Beastliest Couple at Prom. There was even a movement to have a T-shirt made.

On the way home in the limo, Richie once again tried to feel Haley up, only this time, she was too tired and woozy to shove him off. She woke up the following morning, still in the limo, with a pounding headache, a nauseated feeling in her stomach, half her clothes missing and about six dozen photo texts to her phone from people she didn't know, all with the words "Hey, Beast!" in the subject line.

As Haley would learn over the following summer and well into the next school year, it was a difficult nickname to live down.

Hang your head and go back to page 1.

REPORT CARDS ARRIVE

Bad grades can hurt. Badly.

On the day report cards arrived in the mail, Joan easily identified the envelope with the school's return address and opened it excitedly. She had high expectations for her daughter's academic performance in her new school. However, those soon vanished. When Haley got home from hanging out with Irene, Shaun and Devon, her parents were seated at the kitchen table, looking prepared for a very adult conversation.

"Hey," said Haley hesitantly as she approached,

sensing she was about to get a shock. "Is Gam Polly okay?" she asked. "Where's Mitchell?"

"Your grandmother is fine," Perry said sternly. "It's you we're worried about, young lady. Have a seat."

Haley sat down obediently as Perry opened the envelope. "Why don't we start with last year's report card first? 'Haley Miller is an exceptional student. She is attentive, bright and enthusiastic about learning. She is cooperative and a pleasure to have in class. A, A-minus, A, A-plus, A-minus, A.' And now for this year's review." Joan hung her head. Haley knew instantly this was going to be painful. " 'Haley has been tardy twelve times and skipped class altogether six times this semester. She fails to complete homework assignments on time, and she does not participate in class discussion. Haley did not come prepared for her final exams and her grades sorely reflect her lackadaisical attitude toward her schoolwork. C-minus, D, C-plus, D-plus, C, D-minus, F.' "

"Haley," Joan began. Haley noticed that her mom's ears were bright red, which only happened when she was beyond furious. "It says here that you'll have to attend summer school to make up for your poor performance in two classes. I have to be honest with you. I find all this rather hard to believe. This is not the same child who used to stay up until midnight doing extracredit reports." Joan seemed to be getting choked up.

Haley was stunned. Clearly, she'd done far worse in school than she'd thought. *There must be some mistake. I, Haley Miller, have to go to summer school? That's a prison sentence!* The thought of attending classes in the scorching summer heat while everyone else was off vacationing was positively loathsome.

"It's one thing to struggle in school because the work doesn't come easy to you," Perry added. "It's another to just throw your talents away."

As Haley's dad said that, tears started to well up in her eyes.

"Are your friends a bad influence? Is that it?" asked Joan. "I would hate to see you throw your whole education away just to get someone to like you."

Haley had the urge to defend Irene, Shaun and Devon, but she understood why her parents were so upset. She'd made a huge mistake. Gargantuan.

"Mom and Dad," Haley said, coming to an honest realization. "I really like my friends, but you're right, school is too important for me to slack off on my grades. I promise I'll study more and pay better attention. And I'll even try to get Irene, Shaun and Devon more interested in schoolwork too."

"That is not your responsibility, Haley," Perry reminded her. "Those kids can take care of themselves. You have to worry about *you*."

He had a point. But she couldn't not try. Getting Irene, Shaun and Devon interested in schoolwork wouldn't be an easy task. And she didn't know how she would endure the blazing months ahead spent in summer school under Principal Crum's iron-fisted rule with the AC on the fritz. But somehow, Haley decided, she would find a way.

THE END

LIZ RUCKDESCHEL was raised in Hillsdale, New Jersey, where *What If . . .* is set. She graduated from Brown University with a degree in religious studies and worked in set design in the film industry before turning her attention toward writing. Liz currently lives in Los Angeles.

SARA JAMES has been an editor at *Men's Vogue*, covered the media for *Women's Wear Daily*, been a special projects producer for *The Charlie Rose Show*, and written about fashion for *InStyle* magazine. Sara graduated from the University of North Carolina at Chapel Hill with a degree in English literature. She grew up in Cape Hatteras, North Carolina, where her parents have owned a surf shop since 1973.